Beth loves August too much to marry him

"I'd love for you to talk to me about what has hurt you and turned you from God," Beth pleaded. "I'd love to be able to help you through your anger and frustration, but you won't let me. You turn away at every possible opportunity."

"Talking won't resolve anything," August stated firmly.

"And marriage will?"

"I love you, Beth!" August said as he pounded his fist against the table.

"And I love you, August," Beth whispered, ignoring the outburst. "But I can't marry you when your heart isn't right with God. It would always stand between us and eventually divide us. I can't serve two masters, and I won't give up God."

Regina
Borkholder

JANELLE JAMISON is the pen name for Tracie J. Peterson, a very popular inspirational romance writer and regular columnist for a Christian newspaper in Topeka, Kansas.

Books by Janelle Jamison

HEARTSONG PRESENTS

Don't miss out on any of our super romances. Write to us at the following address for information on our newest releases and club information.

Heartsong Presents Readers' Service
P.O. Box 719
Uhrichsville, OH 44683

Destiny's Road

Janelle Jamison

Heartsong Presents

To Bob Ledbetter,
with special thanks
for allowing my hundreds of questions
about the Alaskan Highway
and for his friendship.

ISBN 1-55748-509-7

DESTINY'S ROAD

one

"The Royal Canadian Air Force regrets to inform you
. . ." Bethany Hogan refused to read any further as
the telegram fell from her hand and blew across the
yard.

Chubby four-year-old legs ran across the promise
of new spring grass to catch up with the papers but
were too slow for the job.

Beth watched as two-year-old Phillip followed after his older brother, Gerald. How could she   explain to them that their father had been killed? How
could she hope that they could understand that a
madman named Hitler had made it necessary for their
father to give his life in service to his country?

American-born and native to Alaska, Bethany had
met her Canadian husband only six years earlier in
Fairbanks. He was flying with barnstormers, who for
the outrageous price of two dollars would take individuals up into the air to forget the problems and
concerns of the Depression.

John Brian Hogan, JB to his friends, wasn't
exactly what Beth had been looking for. He was a bit
too wild and carefree, with a love of life that oozed
over into his conversations and chosen profession.
Beth thought him reckless but entertaining.

She remembered standing along the sidelines
watching as her girlfriends took turns flying with
some of the other barnstormers. JB worked for over

an hour, missing several paying customers, in order to coax Beth into the air for free.

It all came rushing back to her as the breeze picked up and blew strong across the open field. The roar of the DH-4's twelve-cylinder engine, the seeming frailty of dope and fabric wings, and the rush of the wind as JB eased back on the stick and the bi-plane became airborne.

Now he was gone. In his passing, two children were left without a father. Bethany squinted against the morning sun and watched as her children came running back across the field. They were laughing, enjoying the moment, the sun, and the excitement of a new day.

"Momma!" Gerald squealed as he wrapped himself around her legs. Phillip mimicked his brother as soon as his little legs could take him to his mother's side.

Beth hugged her children close, refusing to show them her sorrow. *Oh, JB,* she cried silently. *Why? Why did you have to leave them now? Why did you have to leave me?*

"Momma, was that a letter from Daddy?" Gerald asked in his boisterous voice.

Beth steadied her nerves, lifted Phillip into her arms, and led Gerald with her to sit beneath their favorite towering pine. Gerald, always the more sensitive of the two, sobered at his mother's expression. He waited quietly while Beth settled herself with Phillip.

"The letter wasn't from Daddy, but it was about Daddy," Beth said and took a deep breath. She breathed a prayer, asking God for just the right words.

"Daddy has to go away for a long, long time."

"Did he go to heaven?" Gerald asked, surprising Beth with his bluntness.

"Yes," Beth said softly, uncertain that Gerald could really understand. "What made you ask that?"

"Daddy told me he might have to go to heaven instead of coming home after his job was done."

Good old JB, Beth thought. She should have known he would prepare his child for the possibility of his death. "Do you understand about heaven, Gerald?"

"Daddy said it was a really beautiful place. A place where you got to live if you loved God," the boy answered quite seriously.

"That's right," Beth said as she tried to think of what she might say next.

"Will we see him again?"

"Yes," Beth assured. "We'll see him again in heaven."

Phillip seemed oblivious to the news, but Gerald's little forehead furrowed as he concentrated on his mother's answer. Beth wondered if he would cry or if he'd truly be able to grasp the meaning of his father's death. JB had already been gone from Gerald's daily life for several months.

Gerald began to nod his head and Phillip, ever faithful, did likewise. "Then it's okay," he said as he put his hand on his mother's arm. "If Daddy's in heaven, then it's okay."

Beth looked at her brown-eyed son and smiled. "Yes, it's okay, Gerry. Daddy's in heaven and it's really okay."

Phillip squirmed out of Beth's arms and ran after some birds, while Gerald sat beside his mother and held her hand. He seemed to sense that while his mother's words were filled with hope and eternity, her heart was empty and hurting.

Later that night, after Bethany had tucked the boys into the double bed they shared, she made her way to the sitting room. The roll-top desk gave slight resistance as she pushed it open and took a seat.

There was a great deal to be done in order to get everything arranged. Being American, Bethany was determined to return to Alaska and raise her children as Americans, but where should she take them and how would she support them? There was the small nest-egg that she and JB had saved, but that wouldn't last long with two growing boys.

JB had always teased her about being so meticulous and organized. Beth would make lists every fall and again in the spring of all the things that needed to be done. JB thought it foolish, but inevitably he relied upon them every bit as much as his wife. So Bethany made another list; in fact, several.

Across the top of the paper she wrote: *Things to sell. Things to take. Things to do first.* Under the final heading, she listed the thing that seemed most important: *Bury JB.*

Beth worked long into the night, going over the contents of the house and JB's shop. She thought of choice items to save as mementos for the boys, things that would give them fond memories of their father. Glancing up, she noticed the framed picture of JB in his uniform.

She put the pencil down and reached for the picture. For the first time, Beth allowed her tears to fall. It was impossible to imagine that the big-hearted man she'd fallen in love with was gone.

"JB," she said aloud, "you told me this might happen, but I never believed you. You were always able to get out of any scrape no matter how bad." She looked at the photo, tracing JB's outline. He'd obviously been told to look serious for the photograph, but his eyes crinkled with laughter.

"I never, ever thought you'd leave me. I trusted God to keep you in His care, which of course He did. I just didn't know He'd choose to care for you in heaven."

Beth got up from the desk and, with the picture still in hand, stretched out across the couch. She intended only to have a good long cry and then go to bed, but instead she fell asleep clutching the picture to her heart.

"Momma," Phillip patted at Beth's face. "Momma, me eat."

Beth roused herself from a dreamless sleep, grateful for a reason to get up. The picture clattered to the floor, momentarily forgotten as Phillip climbed on top of his mother.

"Come here, you sweet boy," Beth said, pulling the two-year-old into her arms. "You don't look like you need food," she teased as she looked underneath Phillip's nightshirt. "But, you look like you could use a good tickling." Phillip's giggles filled the air as Beth ran her fingers lightly across her son's abdomen.

"Tickle me," Gerald called as he climbed on his mother's legs. "I need tickles, too."

The three of them rolled around the couch, laughing and giggling until Beth felt her sorrow melt away.

JB wasn't really gone. As long as Gerald and Phillip were here, she would have reminders of JB's love for her.

"Come along you ragamuffins," Beth said as she set the boys aside and got to her feet. "I'll get you some breakfast and then we have some errands to do."

The boys padded after their mother to the kitchen and waited impatiently for her to prepare steaming bowls of oatmeal. After placing the food on the table, Beth went to the refrigerator and brought cream for their cereal.

"Berries too, Momma?" Gerald questioned.

"No, I'm sorry. It's still too early for them. I have a little bit of brown sugar, though. I've been saving it just for you two," Beth said as she went to the cupboard and pulled out a small china bowl.

Phillip clapped his hands as Beth spooned the sweetener onto the oatmeal. "Choogar, choogar," he chanted, trying to pick up pieces of the lumpy brown sugar before Beth could blend it in with the cereal.

When breakfast was served, Beth took a seat at the table and she and the boys bowed their heads.

"Father, thank You for the food You've given us," Beth prayed. "We ask for it to nourish our bodies, that we might have the strength and energy to do Your work. Amen."

Gerald and Phillip went to work on their cereal, while Beth pulled a small, worn Bible from the pocket of her apron. Such was their morning routine: breakfast and devotions.

Beth opened to 1 John 2:28 and read to the boys: "'And now, little children, abide in him; that, when he shall appear, we may have confidence, and not be ashamed before him at his coming.'"

She placed the book on the table and turned to Gerald. "Do you understand what that means?"

Gerald got a serious look on his face as his mind struggled to grasp the ancient words. "I know we're little children," he said pointing to himself and then to Phillip.

"That's right," Beth said with a nod. "And 'abide in him' means to live in God and God in you. Do you understand that?" Gerald shook his head yes and Phillip mimicked the action before Beth continued.

"We are all God's little children and this verse tells us that we are to remain close to Him. It also tells us why. It says we need to do this so that we won't be ashamed when God comes back for us."

"Like He came back for Daddy?" Gerald asked, surprising Bethany.

"That's right. Daddy loved God very much, and because Daddy lived close to God, he wasn't ashamed when God told him it was time to come to heaven."

"Daddy in heh, hehbeen," Phillip joined in.

Beth held back her tears. "Yes, Daddy is in heaven and he's smiling right now because his two big boys are learning about God and how much God loves them. It makes your daddy happy and it makes God happy when you spend time learning about the Bible."

"Will Daddy forget us while he's in heaven?" Gerald asked with a look of concern. "What if we don't get there very soon? Will Daddy know us when he sees us?"

Beth couldn't hold back the hot tears that filled her eyes. "Daddy will always remember us. He won't forget us and we won't forget him. You wait here for just a minute," Beth said using the opportunity to wipe her eyes as she went back to the living room for JB's picture.

When she returned to the kitchen, the boys were nearly done with their breakfast. She put the picture in the middle of the table and took her seat. "This picture was taken last year when your daddy went away to fight in the big war."

"He went to fly the airplanes, right, Momma?" Gerald queried.

"Yes," Beth answered. "Your daddy flew the airplanes."

"Did he fly his airplane up to heaven?"

"I'm sure that Daddy was in his airplane when he went to heaven. We never know when God will come to take us home to heaven, so we must always be ready. We must always be good and kind to one another, and we should always live close to God and His Word."

Phillip reached out to the picture. "Daddy?"

Beth grieved that her boys would never remember their father for the person he was. He would only be a character in stories they heard and a friendly face that sat upon their breakfast table.

"Yes, Phillip," she said as she allowed him to hold the picture in his chubby hands, "this is your daddy, and he loved us all very much. Whenever we miss him, we can look at this picture and remember that he doesn't want us to be sad. Can you do that, boys?"

Both boys shook their heads solemnly. They seemed to sense that the moment was quite important. "How long will it be, Momma? How long before we see Daddy in heaven?" Gerald finally asked.

"I don't know, Gerry. But one day we will see him. Of that you can be sure." It seemed to satisfy his boyish curiosity and Beth dismissed them both to play outside.

After cleaning up the breakfast dishes, Beth went once again to the living room where she looked over the lists she had made the previous evening. Taking three thumbtacks, Beth posted her lists to the wall, determined to mark each item off as she accomplished the tasks. She was reaching for the telephone to call Pastor McCarthy when a knock sounded at the front door.

Beth opened it to reveal her closest neighbor and friend, Karen Sawin. Karen was always bubbly and happy-go-lucky, but the look on her face told Bethany that she'd already guessed or heard about the newest telegram.

"I thought you might be able to use a friend," Karen said as she extended a freshly baked loaf of bread.

Beth accepted the still warm bread and ushered Karen into the house. "Thanks. You always seem to know the right thing to do."

"So," Karen started uncomfortably, "I guess you heard something official."

"Yes, JB was killed in action," Beth said matter-of-factly as she put the bread on the coffee table and offered Karen a seat on the couch. "You'll have to forgive the way I look. I fell asleep out here last night and haven't changed clothes."

"Why don't you go ahead and take a nice hot bath and let me keep an eye on the boys?" Karen suggested.

Beth smiled and reached out to take hold of Karen's hand. "You are such a dear friend. I'd really like that, if you don't mind. Afterward, we can have a long talk."

"Of course," Karen said. "Whatever you need."

An hour later, Beth emerged looking refreshed. She'd washed and dried her pale blond hair and gathered it back at the sides with mother-of-pearl combs.

"I feel like a new woman," Beth said as she joined Karen in the living room. She wore a freshly pressed cotton dress whose bright peach color was trimmed with a white eyelet collar and armbands. The matching belt showed off Beth's tiny waistline.

"You look so skinny, Beth. I'll bet you haven't eaten a decent meal since JB. . ." Karen fell silent.

"It's all right, Karen," Beth said as she leaned over to pat her friend's hand. "What's happened has happened. JB is dead. We can't change it by not talking about it."

"You're taking it awfully well. I doubt I would be as capable as you," Karen said honestly.

"I'm not handling it that well, Karen. I'm just numb and reliant upon the Lord."

Karen nodded at Beth's words.

"No doubt in a week or two, I'll be beside myself," Beth continued, "but then again, maybe not. I do have to be strong for the boys—after all, they can't be expected to lose both of their parents."

"That's true," Karen said as she pushed back her dark hair, "and we both know JB wouldn't want you to be sad. I don't think I ever saw JB with a frown on his face."

"Nor me," Beth agreed. "JB was a terminally happy

man. He always joked that St. Peter would meet him at the Pearly Gates and ask him what was so funny. JB did love to laugh."

"I'll never forget the night before he left," Karen remembered. "He was laughing and dancing with everyone, including old Mr. Thompson." Karen stopped short and looked away. "Here I meant to come over and get your mind off JB, and I'm doing just the opposite."

"I know what you mean. I tell myself I don't have to deal with everything at once. I mean, it's been nearly a year since JB joined the service. Aside from his few brief letters, the void has been something I've dealt with in an on-going manner. Yet now that I know he isn't coming back, it seems important to put all our affairs in order and to move on." Beth stared intently into Karen's hazel eyes. "Does that make any sense?"

"I think each person must deal with grief in their own manner. I know I'd be inclined to run away from all of it. Please don't think me unfeeling, Bethany, but I pray to God I never have to know. If something happened to my Miles, I just know I'd crumble."

Beth leaned over and hugged Karen tightly. "I don't think badly of you at all. I pray you never have to know, either. I pray daily that this war will end and Miles will come home safely to you."

"You are such a dear friend, Beth. Is there anything I can do to help you?"

Beth pulled away and got to her feet. "As a matter of fact, there is. I've made several lists." She paused with a grin. "You know me and my lists."

Karen nodded and returned her friend's smile.

"Anyway," Beth continued, "I plan to leave as soon as I can. I want to return to Alaska with the boys and raise them as Americans. After all, they were born in America, and just because their father is—was—Canadian, that doesn't mean they can't share in my heritage as well."

"But where will you go? You haven't any family still living there. Who will take care of you?" Karen questioned in a concerned tone.

"God will take care of me, Karen. Remember Isaiah 54:4-5: 'Fear not; for thou shalt not be ashamed; neither be thou confounded; for thou shalt forget the shame of thy youth, and shalt not remember the reproach of thy widowhood any more. For thy Maker is thine husband; the Lord of hosts is his name; and thy Redeemer the Holy One of Israel; The God of the whole earth shall he be called.' "

"You have a strong faith, Bethany. I'll do whatever I can to help you, but I'll miss you sorely," Karen said as she got to her feet. "Just tell me what I can do."

As spring warmed into summer and the nights grew shorter, Bethany finalized her plans for moving her family to Alaska. She left many of her things with Karen, promising to send for them as soon as she and the boys were settled.

Then, despite the fact that an airplane had claimed the life of her husband, Bethany loaded her boys into the plane of JB's best friend and mentor, Pete Calhoon. With a last look at the place she and JB had called home, Beth turned, resolving to put the past behind her and start a new life in Alaska.

two

Crash! Bang! Julie Curtiss cringed at the sound of the slamming doors. The clamor could only mean one thing: her brother was home, and he wasn't at all happy.

August Eriksson came stomping into the room. Mindless that his heavy boots were covered in mud, August marched across Julie's clean kitchen floor and threw his body against the back of a chair.

"Bad news?" Julie braved the words. Her dark eyes were sympathetic as she reached out to touch her brother's sleeve.

"They said I was too old," August grumbled the words. "I'm not even forty-two, and they think I'm too old to join the military."

Julie bit back a remark about being glad that August couldn't go off to the war in the Pacific. Ever since Pearl Harbor had been bombed the previous winter, August had been bent on participating in the defense of his country.

"A lot of other people are going off and serving," August said, dejected. Although he was two years Julie's senior, he seemed like a little boy to his sister.

"Maybe God has another plan for you, August," Julie suggested as she went to the huge cast iron stove and poured two steaming mugs of coffee.

"I don't think He has any plans for me. I mean, just look at me, Jewels," he said, using his sister's nickname. "Pa died a year ago, and you and Sam took over the house."

"But, August, you asked us to move in here in order to help with the dog kennel," Julie said defensively. "Sam and I can certainly move back to town if you like."

"No. No. No," August said as he ran his fingers through his dark hair. "I didn't mean for you to think that. I would have gone mad if you and Sam hadn't moved in here. It's just, oh, I don't know."

Julie patted August's hand. "I know you want to help fight the war, but August, maybe there's something special for you here in Nome."

"I used to think that, too, but after all these years of being alone except for you, Sam, and Pa, I just want to get out."

"Look, August, it's the middle of the darkest days," Julie said with a glance at the calendar. "It's only the end of March, and with all the darkness we have in the winter, a body is bound to get discouraged."

"It's more than that, Julie. I wanted to have a family. I want to get married and be a father. I want a home of my own, something I can build up with my own hands. I want to have a purpose and be needed by others and to need them in return. I just don't belong here with you and your husband."

"But Sam's your best friend," Julie protested.

"I know, I know, and you're my only living relative. That's my point. I don't want to die without leaving something behind," August answered.

"But if you go off to war and get yourself killed, you won't have a chance to marry and have a family. I can't lie and say I'm not relieved," Julie finally admitted. "When the Nome *Nugget* started reporting the facts of the war, I cringed. I wasn't sure what Sam's response would be, or yours for that matter.

"I cried tears of joy when Sam told me he was too old to go. I'm just as happy to have you stay here, but my heart is broken for your anguish. Please don't hate me for wanting you to stay safe."

"I don't hate you, Julie. I couldn't hate you or anyone else, but right now I'm pretty confused and plenty unhappy," August said and got to his feet. "I'm going for a walk."

"It's awfully cold out there," Julie said and bit her tongue. *No sense in mothering August; he'll only resent it.*

"I know," August said, pulling his parka on. "I shouldn't be too long. Maybe I'll run some of the dogs."

"If you see Sam out there," Julie said, trying to sound disinterested in August's plans, "would you mind sending him my way?"

"Not at all," August replied and started to leave. "Oh, I'm sorry about the mud, Jewels. I can clean it up for you."

"Never mind," Julie said and waved him on. "You just get to feeling better. I'll have some lunch in about an hour."

Julie watched her brother leave in silence. She ached for him and went to the living room determined to pray.

August kicked at the snow as he walked. He'd never known a time in his life when he'd felt so completely useless. Nothing in his life seemed right, and he'd lost all faith in the trust he'd once placed in God.

Forty-one didn't seem all that old to August. He felt vital and young. He could run thirty or more miles a day with his dogs, and he was never sick. How could the army tell him he was too old?

Without realizing what he was doing, August hitched a team of dogs to a sled. He hardly gave the process a second thought as he attached his lead dog first, then swing dogs, team dogs, and finally wheel dogs.

Each dog had his own special talent, and those who were weak were quickly weeded out and put to death. The harsh elements of the north didn't allow for anyone, be they man or beast, to exist without purpose. Perhaps that's why August felt so misplaced and out of sorts. He didn't have any real purpose.

August moved the dogs out without any particular destination in mind. He enjoyed watching the muscular frames of the dogs as they ran with a hearty eagerness.

Many Alaskans had traded in their dogs and sleds for gas-powered snow machines, but August found the dogs more dependable. The machines were always breaking down, and often they were incapable of withstanding the sub-zero temperatures. August reasoned it was impossible to gain warmth from steel and wood if you were stranded in the wilds, but a dog was good to curl up with when the north wind pounded blades of ice into your skin. He'd take his dogs over machines any day.

The dogs worked their way down the roadway to Nome, and when August realized he was nearly at the edge of town, he couldn't decide what to do with himself.

He spoke to no one and didn't offer so much as a wave when people greeted him. He simply anchored his dogs and walked into a nearby café. The look on his face as he pushed back his parka hood was enough to keep people at a distance. Everyone, that is, except his brother-in-law, who entered the restaurant from out of nowhere, on August's heels.

Sam Curtiss ignored August's scowl and motioned the waitress to bring coffee.

"Do you think it will help?" Sam asked, taking a seat opposite August.

"What are you talking about?" August growled.

"Feeling sorry for yourself," Sam said with a grin. "Do you think it will help?"

"If you're here to preach at me, Sam, you can just forget it," August said, refusing to look Sam in the eye.

Sam waited while an older woman poured two cups of thick, black coffee. When she was out of earshot, Sam leaned forward.

"I hadn't planned to preach," he replied. "I just wondered if you were feeling any better."

"No," August answered flatly. "I don't feel any better, and I don't expect talking to you to make any difference."

"Maybe you should give it a try," Sam said, taking a drink. He eyed a questioning look at August.

"Maybe I'd rather be alone," August said firmly. "I don't need you here, Sam. I don't need anybody. The army doesn't want me, women don't seek out my company, and God has apparently deserted me."

"You don't believe that any more than I do."

"I don't know what I believe anymore, Sam."

August stared at the steaming cup for a moment before pushing it away. "I trusted God for a full life, and instead I'm left with an emptiness and void that won't be filled. Why should I go on trusting Him when He's left me to stand alone?"

"Think about your words, August. When you accepted Christ as your Savior, was somebody standing there with a list of prizes? Did you think you'd won the All-Alaska Sweepstakes?"

"Don't be snide with me, Sam. I know God didn't offer me a prize package. He did say, however, that I could ask for anything in the name of His Son. He promised to give me the desires of my heart if I put Him first in my life. So where's the fulfillment of that promise?"

"Your life certainly isn't over, August. Why not be patient and let God guide your steps? It isn't a game of 'I'll give you this, Lord, and You give me that.'"

"I never said it was," August protested as he sank back against his chair.

"Besides, you've had a very good life," Sam reasoned. "Be patient, because God will work a miracle when you least expect it. Just look at your sister and me. I wasn't much younger than you are now when she came into my life.

"I'd been praying most all of my adult life for a Christian wife and although I knew the chances of one coming to me in the wilds of Alaska were slim, God moved. God hasn't left you alone, August. You must have the faith to get beyond this disappointment."

"It's more than the disappointment, Sam. I just

don't know that I can trust God with my heart any more. Things that once seemed clear and inspiring are just rhetoric now."

"Then remember Psalm 37:23-24: 'The steps of a good man are ordered by the Lord: and he delighteth in his way. Though he fall, he shall not be utterly cast down: for the Lord upholdeth him with his hand.' God hasn't deserted you," Sam stressed. "Have faith that He can get you through this dark time, and you'll soon be walking in light again."

August shook his head. "I don't think I care any more."

Sam finished his coffee and stood with a smile on his face. "Oh, you care, August. That's what's grieving you so much. You care because you know the truth of the Word. Once you've tasted the truth, Satan's lies can't guide you into any kind of peace. I'm glad you're troubled and in turmoil right now. I'd be more concerned if you weren't."

"I don't get it," August said as he cast a doubtful look at his older friend. "You're glad I feel this way?"

"I'm not glad that you're hurting, but I'm glad that you're struggling against the feelings that are threatening to bury you. You aren't fighting God, August. You're fighting yourself and what you thought God had planned out for your life. Why not go back to Him and seek the answers you're looking for?"

"What if He doesn't listen?" August questioned softly.

Sam nodded knowingly. "What man hasn't asked himself that question? You've got to believe, August. You've just got to step forward and trust God to be there. Now I'm going home for an overdue lunch. You coming?"

"I guess so," August said as he got to his feet. "There's no reason to sit here."

As August walked out the door of the café, a copy of the local newspaper caught his eyes. "Military Highway To Require Civilian Help," the headline read. August paid the waitress for a copy of the paper and followed Sam into the street.

"Look at this," August said as he scanned the article. "The army is building a road through Canada, the Yukon, and on up to Fairbanks. It says here because of the threat of the Japanese attacking Alaska, the U.S. Government feels it's imperative to have access to the territory."

"There's always water routes and air travel. I can't imagine why they're willing to go to the cost of building a road through the wilderness," Sam said, rubbing his chin thoughtfully.

"Well, the paper says that military sources fear the Japanese might have the capability to deny ships passage through the waterways and that their aircraft would be able to shoot down our military planes. It also says they need civilian forces to help the military units with clearing areas for the road and new airstrips."

Sam noticed excitement in August's voice. "I'd imagine an experienced hand at road building would be a tremendous asset," he suggested quietly.

August looked up from the paper with a grin. "I was just thinking that myself. This road will change Alaska's destiny forever. They're bound to make us a state after this."

"It's an awful long ways off," Sam said, wondering if August was seriously considering the job.

"Maybe it's just the right distance to start a new life," August said as he refolded the paper. "I'm going to do it, Sam. I'm going to go build me a road and change my own destiny."

three

Beth Hogan worked the dough that would soon be delicious loaves of wheat bread. The kitchen already boasted the aroma of wild berry jelly cooking down, and Beth was grateful for the extra warmth of the stove. The day had turned chilly as a mountain thunderstorm hovered in the distance.

Taking a moment from her task, Beth looked out the window to check on her sons. They were playing happily in the back yard, mindless of the threatening storm. At three and five, the boys were growing up almost faster than Beth liked to see.

Glancing past the boys to the mountains that lined the southern horizon, Beth smiled. There had been so much uncertainty when she'd left Canada the previous year, but when she'd stepped from the plane and viewed the panoramic glory, she had declared this piece of Alaska heaven on earth and arranged for a home for herself and her children.

The land hadn't disappointed her, nor had the people. She had been eagerly welcomed into the caring arms of neighbors and new friends, including an elderly woman who most called Granny Gantry.

Granny had a run-down roadhouse, catering mostly to those who traveled the worn path that residents called a road. While spending the winter of 1941 under Granny's protective wing, Beth had learned a great deal.

Day after day, Beth helped to transform the road-house into a prosperous business by adding homey touches. She made rag rugs for the floor and sewed new curtains for the windows. It wasn't long before Beth was even a fair hand at chopping wood and patching walls.

Granny had been pleased with the additional help and company. She seemed to thrive on spoiling the boys by making them special treats. Granny was also a source of Christian fellowship, and Beth relished their times of devotions when the older woman would share her views and knowledge of God.

When Granny passed away suddenly in the spring of '42, Beth again felt the pain of separation. She quickly purchased the property and continued to run the roadhouse, but it wasn't the same without Granny's smiling face.

Shaking off the past, Beth took a deep breath and returned her gaze to the children. They were so little and innocent, but she knew it would only be a heart-beat and they'd be grown. She wondered if they'd be called to war as had so many other mother's sons. She'd already lost a husband to war; would she lose her children, too?

A cold, ominous cloud had settled over the country since the attack on Pearl Harbor, and there wasn't a citizen from Nome to Tok who hadn't felt fear. The entire world was at war, but Alaskans felt the distance between their homeland and the Japanese empire narrow considerably as rumors of impending attacks ran rampant.

Deaths mounted on both sides, each fighting for what they believed to be right. How long would they battle? How many would have to die? No doubt many more would give their lives before the evil that surged throughout Europe and Asia was taken captive and defeated.

Wiping her hands on her apron and seeking to put thoughts of death and war from her, Beth returned to kitchen chores. Business was booming with the arrival of the U.S. Army. They'd come to build a road, a road that everyone said would protect Alaska from the Japanese and one day link the territory to the rest of the world.

Newspapers throughout the nation boasted stories of the undertaking. They likened it to pioneer trailblazing and merited the army with the civilizing of the Alaskan territory. Surveyors were already placing their marks upon the land at Beth's front door.

Now that the national eye was turned upon the rugged wilderness of Alaska, Beth Hogan had little trouble keeping her children fed and clothed. Instead of a roadhouse where people stopped only on their way to somewhere else, Beth found her home becoming a boarding house where customers stayed on a more permanent basis.

The onslaught of new business also helped Beth keep her mind occupied. She still thought of JB and the empty place that his absence had created in her life, but the memories didn't cause her as much pain as they had at first. Sometimes she could laugh or smile at a pleasant memory of her husband.

She kept the picture of JB in a prominent place in the living room, and whenever the boys asked her questions about their father, Beth would try to share bits and pieces of his life.

Just then, Gerald came bursting through the door. "Momma! Momma! Guess what!"

"Calm down, Gerald, and lower your voice," Beth said sternly. She kneaded the bread dough into loaves and placed them in greased pans. "Now take a deep breath and tell me what you're so excited about."

"I saw boats way down the river. Can Phillip and I go to town and see them up close?" Gerald was still panting from the excitement and his run up to the house.

"Absolutely not," Bethany answered. She turned and put the bread in the oven, unaware of the look of disappointment that crossed Gerald's face. "Haven't I told you boys how dangerous the river is? You mustn't go there alone."

"But, it looks like fun, Momma. Please let us go see the boats," Gerald begged.

"No, son. You have to obey me on this because it's very important," Beth said as she knelt beside her five-year-old. "Do you understand?"

"Uh-huh," Gerald replied as he shook his head. "It's 'portant."

"Yes," Beth said as she tousled the child's brown hair. "It's very important. I know you're a big boy and you by yourself might do all right down by the water, but Phillip is too little and he might fall in. As his big brother, it's your job to see to it that he's safe— especially since your father isn't here to watch over him."

"Will Daddy see me watching my brother?"

"I imagine so," Beth said as she straightened up and lifted Gerald into her arms. "I love you both very much. Now, why don't you go outside and keep an eye on Phillip for me?"

"Okay," Gerald said and placed a big kiss on his mother's cheek. "I'll be a big help."

"I'm sure you will be." Beth kissed her son and put him down. As he bounded out the door, her mind filled with worry. Had she said enough to prevent Gerald and Phillip's wanderings? She loved them so much, but then she'd loved JB even more and it hadn't kept him from adversity.

She went back to work with her mind only half on her tasks. She nearly burned the bread and scorched the jam, all the while thinking of how vulnerable her children were. Finally, Beth took herself to her writing desk and pulled out a Bible.

"Lord," she prayed, "I know that worry won't save them, but You can. Father, I can't imagine how You ever sent Your Son, Jesus, to a world You knew would hurt Him. I fear letting my sons from my sight for even a minute. I can't bear the thought that they might get hurt or killed. Please watch over them and care for them. I know JB is in heaven, Lord, and that gives me comfort, but please let me keep my children here with me and let them be safe in my care. Let me be a wise mother, God."

She opened the Bible and scanned Psalm 127:3-5: "Lo, children are an heritage of the Lord: and the fruit of the womb is his reward. As arrows are in the hand of a mighty man; so are children of the youth. Happy is the man that hath his quiver full of them . . ."

Beth smiled, remembering that these verses had been some of JB's favorites. He'd always planned to have a big family or a "full quiver" as he'd often teased.

"These children are gifts from You, Lord," Beth said with confidence. "I place them in Your hands, Father, and I ask for Your protection of them. Amen."

Glancing at her watch, Beth realized that she was falling behind schedule. Leaving her worries at the feet of her Lord, she returned to her list of duties.

Late that May, August arrived in eastern Alaska. He was more than a little anxious about applying for work on the highway. Even though he'd heard they'd take anyone who could work, August still felt the sting of the army's earlier rejection and wondered if the rumors were true.

August gazed across the valley where rows of tents had been erected to house the army. Beyond these were olive-drab vehicles and heavy construction equipment. The entire landing buzzed with activity while soldiers and civilians rushed to accomplish the business of the day.

After questioning one of the passing soldiers, August made his way to the tent of the commanding officer.

"You need to speak with the area supervisor of the U.S. Public Roads Administration," the officer told August. "I'm certain, however, that you won't be idle for long. We can use every man we can get."

"Glad to hear it," August said and got up to leave. "I'm anxious to get to work."

"Then you're in the right place," the man said from behind his make-shift desk. "You can find the supervisor at the airfield. While we're clearing this path, we're also laying out new landing strips. Just follow the river to the crossroads and turn right. It's just a half mile or so from there. Like I said, you shouldn't have any trouble getting a job."

"Thanks again for your help," August said and left in search of the airfield.

As August walked the short distance down the river to the crossroads, he noticed how different the land was from his native Nome. The fertile valley made Nome seem barren. Tall spruce, fir, and pine weaved a rich green pattern across the land. Wildflowers and carefully tended gardens were visible reminders of the sun's power in a land that enjoyed over eighteen hours of light each day.

August had already been told of cabbages weighing nearly forty pounds and of cucumbers that were longer than a man's arm and nearly as wide around. It was a land of many wonders, and August was only beginning to learn of its richness.

The hike to the airfield did him good, and August breathed deeply of the storm-chilled air. All morning, thunder had rumbled in the distance, but the storm seemed to hang in suspended indifference over the snow-capped mountains.

As August approached the airfield, he discovered that it was hardly more than a cleared path. At one end a windsock had been erected on a pole, and at the other end several tents and wooden buildings stood in sorry contrast to the grandeur of the landscape.

"Excuse me," August said as he approached a mechanic. The man was working on a large tractor, cursing and throwing tools as he did so.

"Whadyawant?" the man asked, garbling the words together.

"I wondered where I might find the supervisor for the Public Roads Administration," August replied.

"Over there," the man said, motioning to the nearest tent.

August thanked the man and walked toward the tent. Suddenly, an older man charged out, nearly colliding with August.

"Sorry, I wasn't paying attention. What can I do for you?"

"I'm looking for work on the road," August explained.

"We can use you," the man said enthusiastically. "Come on inside and we'll talk. Have you any particular job experience that might help us decide where to place you?"

"I can operate most of the machinery," August admitted. "I helped to build roads in Nome."

"So you know the problems we're facing with the permafrost," the man spoke without waiting for August to reply. "We have approximately eighty days between frosts and little more. Even at that, a foot beneath the surface the ground is always frozen solid."

"I know the dilemma well," August said.

"The army is in charge of the road, although the Roads Administration has some control because we work in cooperation with one another. Right now, a big part of our civilian effort is aimed at meeting the need for a bigger airfield.

"Our problem is the complications with ground thaw and boggy surface water. Do you think you can render any new thoughts on the matter? With you being an experienced road builder in these conditions, I think you might have a suggestion or two that we haven't considered."

"I'd be happy to offer whatever knowledge and experience I have. I'm too old for the army, or I'd be off defending our country in the war, so I'm open to whatever you have for me," August answered.

"Great. You can start tomorrow. Be here at six and I'll show you around."

"I'll be here," August said as he followed the man outside. "Where can I find sleeping accommodations?"

"That's a good question," the man said as he thoughtfully considered the matter. "I take it you didn't bring a tent with you."

"Nope," August said with a sheepish grin. "I figured you folks were more civilized over here."

"Don't include me in the folks from these parts. I'm from Oklahoma, and this country's a whole sight different from what I'm comfortable with. Your best bet is to ask around town. Some of the folks are bound to have an idea."

"I guess that'll have to do," August said with a nod.

"Wish I could offer you more help, but I've only been here a week, myself."

"No problem. By the way, I'm August. August Eriksson."

"Good to meet you," the man said and extended his hand. "I guess we're a little lax on formalities around here. I'm Ralph Greening, the area supervisor for the U.S. Public Roads Administration."

August shook the man's hand, and after renewing his promise to return at six the next morning, he made his way back to town.

At the crossroads, August noticed that the storm had dissipated and moved to the east. The clouds cleared out to make the vibrant colors of the landscape come alive.

August enjoyed the breeze through his dark hair and the scent of pine as it penetrated his senses. He marveled at the blackness of the glacier silt dirt and wondered at the stories he'd heard of a glacier's ability to physically move its location as much as ten feet a day.

Before he turned to head back to town, August paused long enough to glance down the picturesque winding road. *It might be a good place to call home,* he thought.

A child's shrill scream filled the air and caught August's attention. He listened again, thinking it came in the direction of town, but soon realized it came from down the road in the opposite direction. The intensity of the child's cry for help sent August in a full run down the riverbank.

Gerald Hogan stood on the small wooden bridge that crossed the river nearly a quarter of a mile from his home. "Help! Help!" he screamed. "My brother can't swim."

August arrived in time to see a small, brown-haired child slip beneath the churning water. Without thought for his own safety, August rushed into the river and swam with the current to catch up to the flailing form.

The icy water bit into August's skin as he maneuvered himself better to take hold of the little boy. He stretched out his hand as the child came within reach, only to hit a boulder. The impact sent him careening away.

August knew he'd have to fight with all his strength to once again reach the drowning boy. He lunged forward in the water and grabbed hold of the boy's collar, pulling the child back against his chest.

Fighting the current, August moved toward shore where the water was considerably more shallow. He pulled the sputtering, crying child with him. Once he reached the riverbank, August fell back against it, breathing hard. Every muscle in his body ached from the stress and cold, but the child was crying and that meant he was alive.

"Are you my daddy?" Gerald asked from over-head.

"What?" August asked in surprise. Drenched and freezing, he was certain he'd misunderstood the boy's question.

"You are my daddy!" Gerald yelled with exuberance. "Mommy! Mommy!" He ran off in the direction of home before August could stop him and set him straight.

Getting to his feet and cradling the cold, crying boy to his chest, August followed in the direction Gerald had disappeared.

"Mommy, come quick. It's Daddy!" Gerald yelled as he ran through the roadhouse front door.

Beth came rushing from the back room. "What are you saying, Gerald?"

"Phillip fell in the river, and Daddy jumped in after him." The excitement in Gerald's voice left Beth little doubt about the truth of his statement.

"Take me to where Phillip is," Beth said without thought of reprimanding the disobedience of her sons.

"Hurry, Gerry. Take me to your brother."

"He's all right, Momma," Gerald said as he led the way. "Daddy came back. Daddy saved Phillip!"

Beth shook her head, unable to understand. "Daddy is in heaven," she said as she took hold of Gerald's eager hand.

"I know, but you said this was heaven," Gerald stated. "Remember? You said this was heaven when we moved here. I knew my Daddy would come home."

Beth's heart ached. How could she explain the misunderstanding to her excited five-year-old? She was torn. She had to assure herself that Phillip was safe and alive, but she was also concerned that Gerald accept the truth of his father's death.

Taking her eyes from her son, Beth lifted her gaze to see a dark-haired man approaching down the road. Her breath caught in her throat and her heart beat faster. From a distance, she could almost believe that JB was walking toward her.

Beth stopped in her tracks, while Gerald pulled at her arm. "Come on, Mommy. It's Daddy and Phillip," he insisted.

Beth let go of Gerald and held her hand to her throat. She paled at the ghostly image of her husband. The same dark hair and medium build. The same self-confident stride. Pushing aside such thoughts, Beth rushed forward to take Phillip.

"Daddy saved Phillip from the river," Gerald announced.

Phillip had wrapped his arms around August's neck and as Beth reached out to take him, Phillip resisted.

"No. Want Daddy," he said firmly.

Beth looked into the dark eyes of the man who'd saved her child. She wanted to explain, to say something that would answer the question in the man's eyes, but words wouldn't come.

"You're freezing," Beth finally managed. "Come with me, and I'll get you something dry to wear."

August nodded and followed Beth back to the roadhouse. She paused to open the door with trembling hands, allowing August to pass through with Phillip. "Thank you," she whispered as August moved only inches from her.

He turned his face to meet her pale blue eyes. He saw the concern for her child and something else. August began to realize that he represented an image from her past.

"You're welcome," he whispered.

four

Phillip refused to be fussed over, and Beth watched in silent concern for signs of complications. The boy seemed fine, however, and the only real dilemma was how to explain to him that the man to whom he clung so affectionately wasn't his father.

Beth moved uncomfortably around the room as she built up the fire in the stove and retrieved warm towels for August and Phillip. It was hard to allow the stranger such an intimate role in her son's life, but at the moment she didn't know what else she could do.

"I must apologize for my sons' behavior," Beth finally said, noting the confused expression on August's face. "The boys' father was killed last year in the war. They have a misconception about his coming back, or, well, that's not really where the misunderstanding occurred, but it's a long story."

She reached out and pried Phillip from August's lap. "I can offer you a robe while your clothes dry," Beth said, turning to leave the room. "I'll have Gerald show you where you can change."

August nodded and watched as the petite woman placed a kiss on her son's forehead. He noted the relief in her eyes and the gratitude. He admired the way she handled herself in the midst of the crisis and the tender way she mothered her children. He was so absorbed in watching her as she left the room that he barely heard Gerald's little voice as he instructed August to follow him.

The boy offered August the robe and turned to leave. "I'm glad you came home, Daddy. I missed you."

"Son, I'm not your daddy, but if I were, I'd love having a big strong boy like you," August said with a smile.

"You're not my daddy?" Gerald questioned.

"No," August said offering the boy his hand, "but I'd like to be your friend. I just moved here and I don't have any friends. Would you be my friend?"

Gerald wrinkled his forehead as he often did when considering something important. "I wanted you to be my daddy. You look like my daddy." He paused in thoughtful contemplation before adding, "I guess I can be your friend."

"I'd sure like it," August said as he pulled the wet shirt from his body. "Now why don't you go see if you can give your mommy some help while I change out of these clothes." Gerald nodded and left August to contemplate the situation.

"Momma," Gerald said as he came into his bedroom.

Beth looked up from where she was putting dry clothes on Phillip. She'd already checked his body for injuries that had been missed before, but other than a few scrapes and bruises, Phillip had fared rather well. God had certainly been watching over him, even sending the stranger who so closely resembled JB.

"What is it, honey?"

"That man says he's not my daddy. I thought he was my daddy, but he isn't."

Beth lifted Gerald into her arms and hugged him close. "No, he's not your daddy. Honey, Daddy is never coming back. Not here. Not on earth. Heaven is where he lives now, and he's going to stay there forever.

"Someday, we'll all leave this earth and go to heaven, but when that happens, Gerald, we can't come back here. We won't even want to. Daddy is happy in heaven, and he won't ever come back here, but someday we'll see him again. Do you understand that?"

"I understand," Gerald said with surprising acceptance. "I told that man I'd be his friend. Is that all right?"

"Of course you can. Now, you two play in here while I fix some lunch for everyone. I'm counting on you to behave," Beth said, kissing each of them.

"We be good," Phillip said, causing Beth to smile.

"I'll call you when lunch is ready," she said and turned to go.

"Can my new friend have lunch with us?" Gerald asked innocently.

Beth nodded. "I'll ask him right now."

Beth was already busy with lunch preparations when August came into the kitchen with his wet clothes.

"Here," Beth said as she put down the potato she was washing. "Let me take those and hang them out back."

"I hate to be a bother," August said with a grin. There was something about the small woman that captivated him. She seemed so alive and energetic, and August found it hard to believe that she'd never remarried.

Beth glanced up as she took the clothes, and her heart nearly stopped. August's grin was so like JB's. "I suppose," she murmured, forgetting the lunch invitation, "I should introduce myself. I'm Bethany Hogan."

"I'm August Eriksson. May I call you Bethany?"

"Please, or Beth if you prefer."

"I like the name Beth. I hope you will call me August."

Beth nodded and shifted the dripping clothes. "I'm grateful for what you did. Saving my son's life must have taken an incredible act of bravery. I thank God you were there when he needed you." Before August could reply, Beth quickly moved through the kitchen and out the back door.

She pinned the clothes to the line, cherishing the once familiar weight of a man's clothing. She ran her hand across the collar of August's shirt.

August stood just inside the doorway, hoping that Beth wouldn't see him. He watched as she seemed lost in the moment and wondered if she would ever put her dead husband to rest.

When she turned back toward the peeled log house, August ducked back and quickly took a seat at the kitchen table. He pretended to be preoccupied with his own thoughts when Beth returned to finish fixing lunch.

"I hope you like fried potatoes and ham," Beth said as she continued with her work. "I've also got canned peaches and fresh bread."

"Sounds wonderful, but I hadn't intended on staying for lunch. I never meant to intrude," August said softly.

"Intrude? You saved my son's life. Your presence here is anything but an intrusion. Lunch is an inadequate payment for such a deed."

"Maybe you could tell me where I might find a place to stay," August requested. "I've just arrived from Nome, and I have a job lined up with the Public Roads Administration. I'm not at all familiar with the area, however, so I need some suggestions."

Beth smiled and allowed a bit of a laugh to escape. "It would seem God threw us together for more than one purpose," she mused. "Northway doesn't offer much in the way of accommodations. I run this as a roadhouse, and I just happen to have lost a boarder this morning. I have a small room with a bed, washstand, and dresser. I don't offer regular meals, what with the rationing and all, but the room rates are reasonable."

"Sounds great," August said enthusiastically. Here was the perfect opportunity to stay close by and learn more about this young widowed mother. He cocked his head toward the stove with a chuckle. "What about lunch?"

"What about it?"

"You said no meals."

Beth laughed in spite of herself. "Well, occasionally I offer a meal or two for special deserving souls."

"If it's half as good as it's starting to smell, I'll try extra hard to be deserving. Besides, where else am I going to find such pleasant company?"

Beth shook her head with a smile. What kind of man was this August Eriksson? He stormed into their lives, saving her child from certain death, and now he sat as relaxed and easy-going as if they were life-long friends sharing a passing moment.

"What are you smiling about?" August asked as he leaned forward.

"What?" Beth realized she'd betrayed her amusement with the situation and wasn't quite sure how to explain.

"I saw that smile," August answered. "It's a very nice smile, if I might add."

Beth turned back to her work and changed the subject. "What prompted you to move here from Nome?"

August shrugged his shoulders and leaned back. "I heard about the road project, and I wanted to be part of it. I was too old for the army, and I wanted to do something worthwhile with my life—something that would show after I was gone."

Beth nodded. "That sounds reasonable. Did you leave your family in Nome?"

"I don't have any family," August said and then corrected himself. "Except for my sister and her husband. My father passed away last year, and I've never married."

"I see," Beth said stirring the cut potatoes into the hot lard on top of the stove. She turned thick ham steaks in the cast iron skillet, satisfied with the way they were browning.

"What about you? Any family other than the boys?" August questioned curiously.

"No, there's no one else," Beth answered. She retrieved canned peaches from the cupboard before continuing. "My husband, JB, was a pilot with the Royal Canadian Air Force. He was killed shortly after the Battle of Britain."

"I'm sorry," August whispered. "What happened?"

"His best friend wrote me about it," Beth said and realized it was the first time she'd ever shared the details of JB's death. "JB was one of the best pilots in the service. He always managed to get himself and his plane out of any risky situation, except the last time. JB always had a bad feeling about using anybody else's plane. Sure enough, when he died, he was flying another man's Spitfire in a routine maintenance check."

"Was he shot down?" August asked, intent on the young woman's answer.

"No," Beth said, remembering the words of the letter she'd received. "He took off but didn't have enough power to make the Spitfire climb. He reached the end of the runway with a forest of trees directly in front of him and not enough lift to clear them. He crashed into them and was killed instantly in an explosion."

"How awful," August said considering the fiery death.

"My comfort is that JB was a devout Christian. He loved the Lord more than anything in this world, and I have confidence that he's in heaven."

August grimaced slightly at Beth's reference to JB's devotion to God. He'd once felt that way about God himself. Now there was only bitter resentment for what he'd lost out on.

"What's wrong?" Beth questioned, noticing August's frown.

"Nothing," August replied as he tried to change the subject. "Your boys must have been very young. No wonder they thought I was their father."

Beth realized she'd hit a nerve with August. "They

were very young when JB joined the service and went away. I've tried to keep his memory alive by telling them stories of their father and keeping his picture in the living room, but it isn't the same. I worry about them sometimes, but when I get too concerned, I pray about it and turn them over to their heavenly Father." Beth wondered how August would react to another reference to God.

August didn't have a chance to respond, however, as Gerald called from the other room, "Is it time to eat yet?"

Beth watched August's expression change to one of amusement. "Sounds like I'm not the only one who's hungry," he chuckled.

"I'll be right back," Beth said after giving the potatoes a quick stirring. She disappeared for a moment and returned with the boys right behind her. "You boys take a seat with Mr. Eriksson at the table, and we'll eat."

"Would it be all right if they called me August?"

Beth nodded. "I suppose, if that's your wish."

"It is," August said with a smile. "Would you boys like that?"

"August is a month," Gerald offered as if it were news to the stranger.

"That's right, and you are every bit as smart as you are brave. I imagine your mother is very proud of you."

Gerald beamed from ear to ear, while Phillip leaned over and reached for August's hand. "Daddy," he stated clearly, refusing to have any part of August's first name.

Gerald reached over and pulled his brother back.

"No, Phillip, he's not our daddy, but maybe he will be." Gerald looked up at his mother and asked, "Do you think since our real daddy isn't coming back that August could be our new daddy?"

Beth turned crimson at the question, and August fought to keep from revealing his own consideration of such an idea. He was already more than just a little fond of the young mother and her boys. Still, they'd only met, and August knew there was much more to be considered than physical attraction.

"Why don't you just pray about it, Gerry," Beth finally suggested. "God will listen to your prayers, and if He feels that it's important for you to have a new daddy, then He will send one to us."

"I did pray for a daddy," Gerald insisted. "I prayed that God would send Daddy home, but you told me he has to stay in heaven. So maybe God sent this one instead." He pointed at August and smiled. "I think you'd make a good daddy."

"I think you're right," August said with genuine fondness for the boy. "Maybe I could be a pretend daddy," he offered with a glance toward Beth. "If your momma doesn't mind, maybe I could take you boys fishing and teach you how to chop wood and hunt for food. Of course, I have to work at my job with the new highway, but when I'm not working, maybe we could do some things together."

Gerald clapped his hands and bobbed up and down in his seat. At his brother's excitement, Phillip squealed with delight and Beth had no idea how to react. She thought it totally inappropriate for August to even suggest such a thing, while the boys thought it perfectly natural.

Unable to hold back her tears, Beth turned quickly to the food on the stove to avoid worrying the children or causing August to question her reaction. Regaining her composure, she wiped the tears with her apron and joined her family at the table with the steaming food. She started to sit and then remembered the peaches and bread.

"So is that okay, Momma?" Gerald questioned. "Can August be our pretend daddy?"

Beth turned to meet August's dark eyes. He seemed to understand her pain and offered a warm smile that reassured her that his intentions were only those that would benefit her sons.

"It's okay, Gerry. You and Phillip can probably learn a lot from August, but just remember to tell me your plans first." She said the latter for August's sake more than the boys. He nodded a promise and Beth felt calmness wash over her.

She opened the can of peaches and poured them into a bowl, then cut thick slices of her slightly over-browned bread. Bringing these to the table along with the jelly dish, Beth took her seat.

"Would you like to offer grace, August?" Beth questioned, wondering what his response would be.

August shook his head. "I'd like to hear Gerald give grace, if you don't mind."

Beth nodded, thinking how smoothly August had avoided having to pray.

"Dear God," the boy began, "this is Gerald Hogan. You have my daddy in heaven with You, and I want You to tell him that August is going to be our pretend daddy. Tell him we still love him, but we need a daddy on earth."

Gerald's words cut deeply into Beth's heart. She'd tried so hard to be mother and father to her sons and never once thought of the void in their lives.

"And God," Gerald continued as an afterthought, "thanks for the food. Amen."

Beth opened her eyes to find August's gaze fixed upon her. She returned the stare while the boys, mindless of the exchange, helped themselves to bread and jelly.

Beth's expression was almost one of pleading, August decided, but for what? Was she fearful that he'd hurt her young boys, or was she more frightened of how his "pretend fatherhood" might affect her? She looked so young and scared. August wished he could ease her worries.

Without thought, he reached out and placed his hand over hers and gave a squeeze. Then just as quickly, August turned his attention to the food and found himself in an intense conversation with Gerald about the new highway.

A strange sensation crept over Beth. Her heart pounded at the thought of August touching her, yet her mind screamed betrayal. She mindlessly pushed her food around the plate, all the while considering the implication of August's role playing. It seemed such a reasonable arrangement, yet for all she was worth, Bethany couldn't comprehend why.

five

August's work with the Alaskan/Canadian Military Highway project took him away from Beth and the boys for long hours each day. Often when he arrived home it was all he could do to clean up before dropping into bed. Gerald and Phillip grew impatient for his company, but Beth faithfully explained why it was necessary for August to spend so much time away from them.

The combined efforts of the United States and Canada resulted in the scheduled creation of a highway that would cover more than 1,486 miles from Dawson Creek, British Columbia, to Fairbanks, Alaska. Calling it a highway was an optimistic overstatement. The road was clearly nothing more than a bulldozed path through an unyielding wilderness.

Never intended to do more than provide emergency access to the north should the Japanese cut off the water and air routes, this road of mud and ice quickly became a problem of outrageous proportions.

Frozen sub-soil, permafrost, muskeg, and long hours of sunlight created problems that made engineers throw up their hands in frustration. Coupled with the fact that there were inadequate supplies and living accommodations for the eleven thousand troops, most of whom were from the southern United States and completely unacquainted with the cold temperatures that seemed to come at will, the highway quickly became a matter of man against nature.

Canada provided access to the lands through British Columbia and the Yukon Territory, as well as much of the needed building materials. All of this was given in exchange for unlimited use of the road following the war.

As engineers and administrators brought their plans together and fine-tuned the design of the project, it was determined that over 130 log and pontoon bridges would be needed to accommodate the hundreds of rivers and lakes that the highway would have to cross.

Added to this were some eight thousand culverts to be dug and reinforced to combat the constant drainage problems created by the swampy soil.

Behind the frustrations of a seemingly endless number of new problems was the threat of Japanese invasion of Alaska. Though few knew of the plan, military experts had found a way to decode Japan's messages in time to learn of Alaska's vulnerability to attack.

Even as far north as the rural villages of Alaska, and perhaps because such vulnerability seemed evident, the mood was one of hushed and guarded silence.

Beth's ten-room boarding house was rapidly becoming a common meeting place for the army leadership and the Public Roads Administration. If the weather was cooperative, the group usually assembled outside, where August had placed a number of crudely built tables and chairs. Other times, however, the weather was rainy or cold, and Beth allowed the men to take over her living room while she and the boys held up in her bedroom.

Glancing outside, Beth could see that the day's weather would allow for an outdoor gathering, and she breathed a sigh of relief. The meetings always made her rather uncomfortable. She never could figure out what disturbed her most: the presence of uniformed men, or the worry that military secrets might fall upon the ears of her children, only to be carelessly babbled later.

She finished pulling the last of five wild raspberry pies from the oven as August came striding into the room.

"Ummm, smells wonderful, Beth. Don't suppose you're going to let me buy them for our meeting?"

"What else would I do with five pies?" Beth asked, chuckling. "Are you certain the men will reimburse you? I can't charge you two dollars a pie in good faith if I have to worry that you'll be out the entire amount."

"They stand in line to pay me," August said with a grin and added, "and at thirty cents a slice, they're going out in good shape, and so am I. Helps me pay the rent," he teased.

"I keep meaning to talk to you about that," Beth said as she smoothed back her blond hair and reinserted one of the combs that held it back at the sides.

"Great," August said in a mocking tone of dissatisfaction, "I suppose my rent is about to go up."

"No, not at all," Beth said, mortified that August would tease about such a thing.

"Relax, it was a joke, Beth," August said as he eyed the young woman seriously. "What did you want to talk about?"

"I can't see you having to pay as much as everyone else when you help out so much around here. I mean, you cut 'most all my wood, you mended the fence and the roof, not to mention that you worked up the dirt for my garden. It's only fair that I offer you some type of compensation."

August smiled and wondered if Beth could begin to imagine the type of compensation he'd like to redeem from her. The fact was he was growing more attracted to the young widow and her sons each day.

"I'm sure we can work something out," August finally said. "But if you're doing it for my sake, then stop worrying. I'm grateful for the time you allow us to meet and disrupt your home in order to coordinate plans for the road."

"I don't feel it's adequate compensation," Beth interjected. "I'd like to at least reduce your rent. If you have something else in mind, I'm open to suggestions."

August grinned and pushed back his black hair. "Well, an occasional hot meal might do the trick," he said, knowing that he couldn't very well come out and say that he'd like to spend more time getting to know her.

"That seems a simple request," Beth said, realizing how pleasant it would be to have August at her table. "But not an occasional meal. I think it's only right that you share all our meals, if you want to. I'll even pack you a lunch if you'd like."

"You'll spoil me," August laughed, "but I'll enjoy it while you do. I'd be quite happy to accept your offer, Bethany."

Beth smiled nervously and made a scene of rechecking the oven as if a pie had been inadvertently overlooked. She knew that August was attracted to her, yet she hadn't decided if she liked the idea or not.

It had been over a year since JB had died, and longer than that since she'd seen him, but the ghostly image of her husband was never so haunting as when Beth felt the cold, gold band that still adorned her finger. Perhaps when she was ready to put away that last reminder of her marriage, she would be able to deal with the interest of another man.

"Well, I'd best make sure everything is ready for our meeting. The army's bringing the coffee this time, so we shouldn't have any trouble staying awake long enough to resolve any new differences. I'll be back for those pies in about an hour, if that's all right with you."

"They should be cooled by then," Beth said and offered August a smile.

August nodded and left Beth to the task of cleaning up. Beth watched through the window as several army vehicles pulled into her yard, unleashing a throng of uniformed men and a large coffee pot.

A knock on her front door sent Beth to answer it. She opened the door to find two young soldiers looking rather sheepishly at her.

"May I help you?" she questioned softly.

"Ma'am, we're here helping with the road," one of the men began as if Beth wouldn't already be privy to the information.

Beth nodded and the man continued.

"Well, me and Ronnie here, we've been coming

to these meetings, and well, ma'am," he stammered for just the right words.

"Go on," Beth encouraged sweetly.

"Well, it's like this. We've been eating your cakes and pies whenever Mr. Eriksson offers them for sale, and we surely do miss our mom's cooking. Army grub just ain't anywhere near as good."

"I'm sure that's true," Beth said suppressing a laugh.

"We was wondering, hoping really, that we could pay you to make some of our favorite sweet potato pie. We've managed to get our hands on some canned sweet potatoes, and while they won't be near as good as fresh, we'd be mighty happy to pay you to bake us however much it would make. In the way of pies that is."

Beth felt sorry for the boys. "I'm not sure I have a recipe for sweet potato pie," she said honestly.

"It's pert near the same as pumpkin," the other boy offered. "But I reckon I can get you a copy of the recipe from somebody."

"Well then, you get me the recipe, and I'll be happy to make your pies. One thing though, I use mostly honey, due to the shortage of sugar. If you don't think the results will be as good, we'd probably best call off the whole arrangement right now."

"No ma'am," the first soldier offered. "Whatever way you make it will be just fine. We'll be back when we can bring you the recipe and the sweet potatoes. How much you gonna charge us for the pie?"

Beth thought for a moment. "I think a dollar would be a fair amount," she answered. While she charged August two dollars for most of her pies and cakes, she knew he easily made his money back. These boys, however, were not going to be making much profit because Beth was certain they'd be eating most of the pie themselves.

"Sounds just fine by us," the one called Ronnie said as he looked at his friend. "They charge us nearly that much for a single piece at the café in town, and the army could never make anything as good as what you serve, ma'am."

"Well, I appreciate your compliments, boys. Now you'd best get around back, because I've a feeling the meeting will be starting shortly, and tonight we're having raspberry pie."

"Yes, ma'am!" they answered in unison and hurried to the back yard.

"So our biggest problem at this point," Ralph Greening was explaining, "is the need for a much larger airfield in order to bring in the bigger planes and more supplies."

"It's not just a problem," an army colonel offered. "It's imperative that we have this runway."

"I understand the need, gentlemen. However, the land around us is most uncooperative. We have a tremendous problem with the permafrost. I've asked August Eriksson to address this problem and to let you know about the progress we've made. August, go ahead."

"As we've cleared land for the runway and grated the sphagnum moss from the topsoil, we've run into the constant problem of ground thaw. The moss has always acted as an insulator that keeps the sub-soil frozen and firm. When the moss is removed we get a swamp."

"But we have to have that runway," the colonel insisted.

"I realize that colonel, and if you'll hear me out, I'll explain how we're combatting this situation. By experimenting we've come up with a plan that seems to be working. First, we skim off the top-soil and moss, allowing the ground to thaw. When this next layer of ground has completely warmed up, we grate off another portion and allow this section to thaw as well. We do this over and over until what we have is an excavation several feet deep.

"Next, we fill this area with sand from the river bottom. This sand allows the sub-soil waters to rise to the level of the surrounding ground's water table. Then, due to the freezing temperatures of the soil, this water freezes and becomes a rock solid surface, while the sand acts as an insulator. This should then allow us to put the regular asphalt apron on top and leave the surface fixed and sturdy year-round."

"Ingenious," the colonel said, offering his first positive word. "Has it been tested?"

"Yes," August replied, feeling rather proud of himself. "It has and with the exact results we'd hoped for. Our only holdback is waiting for each process of ground thaw. Other than that, we would have the main runway completed in a very short time."

"Might the usage of steam from a portable boiler speed up this process?" the colonel questioned.

"That is a possibility," August said with a nod toward Ralph Greening. "I'm sure my supervisor would be happy to discuss the matter with you."

"Most assuredly," Ralph answered.

"I believe," the colonel said with thoughtful

consideration, "we could offer the use of such army equipment when it's not being used for other purposes. Will you have enough manpower for the job?"

"We've hired many of the locals for additional help," Ralph Greening added. "We're paying a dollar an hour, so pass the word among the civilians as you're out among them. The more hands we have, the quicker the project will be completed, and we'll be able to get those big transport planes in here."

"The Northwest Transport Command will be grateful for that," the colonel said as he sat back in the chair for the first time.

"I'm sure many of the Ta'nana people will be happy to help," one of the local men who'd been working with August spoke up. "I know these Indians, and they are good people."

"We'll take them all," Ralph said. "Anybody and everybody. If we're to have this road in place by fall, we can't be picky about who works and who doesn't."

"Well, I'd say the situation is well under control," the colonel remarked. "Now, how about one of those delicious desserts that Mrs. Hogan makes for us?"

August smiled and got to his feet. "It's raspberry pie tonight, and you all know the price. Just take up the collection, and I'll borrow a couple of your men to help me bring out the goods."

Instantly the men began reaching into their pockets. As a hat was passed, the money was eagerly handed over. August grabbed the nearest two men and quickly returned with the five pies. The hat was passed to August, as the men gathered around waiting patiently for their pie. Shortly after the food was gone and the coffee drained, the meeting ended and the satisfied men returned to their tents for some much-needed sleep.

August counted out ten dollars for Beth and pocketed the other two. He was tired, but grateful that it was Saturday. He'd managed to wrangle the following day off and hoped that somehow he'd talk Beth into a picnic with the boys. He was considering just how he might ask her, when Beth appeared to reclaim her pie tins.

"Looks like the meeting was successful," Beth said as she stacked the pans.

"Yes, very," August agreed and added, "Do you have to rush right back?"

The light was fading, and in the twilight that filtered through the tall birch and spruce trees, Beth's face seemed shrouded in the shadows. Still, August could see that she liked the idea of remaining.

"I can stay for a little while, although I hate to keep you up," Beth said, putting the pans down and taking the seat across from August.

"That's one of the reasons I asked you to stay," August replied. "I have tomorrow off and hoped that maybe you would agree to picnicking with the boys and me."

"That sounds like a lot of fun," Beth admitted. "Perhaps you would accompany us to church first." She knew August avoided any reference of such things, but she wanted to find out why he was hesitant when it came to God.

To August's own surprise, he agreed to go. "I suppose that would fall into line."

"Church is at eleven, so you should be able to sleep late. I'll try to keep the boys quiet."

"No, don't," August answered. "I want to get up early and play with them."

"I appreciate the way you look after them. I've never seen them so happy. They care quite deeply for you," Beth said softly. "I hope you realize how much they adore you."

"I do," August said and leaned forward. "Does that worry you?"

"I suppose it does," Beth replied. "They suffered the loss of their father, and then I uprooted them and moved them here. They need to feel secure about their home and the people they care about."

"Do you think I'm incapable of offering them stability in our friendship?" August questioned seriously.

"Not really," Beth said thoughtfully. "I suppose my real concern is that soon the road will be completed and you'll be on your way. I know that would be devastating to them."

"Who says I'll be on my way? If I have something to stick around for, I can't see giving that up," August whispered in a low, husky voice. He wondered if Beth would understand his meaning.

"I think as long as you want a reason to stay, you'll have one. The boys are devoted to you, and I want . . ." Beth grew uncomfortable and got to her feet. "I'd better clean up this mess."

August got up and moved behind Beth. "I'd rather hear you finish that thought."

Beth could feel his warm breath against her neck as August spoke. She wanted very much to get away from the loneliness that threatened to strangle her, but she was also afraid of the feelings that were building in her heart.

"I'm not sure it would be wise," Beth finally whispered.

August very gently turned her to face him. He gazed deep into her eyes just before he lowered his lips to press a gentle kiss upon Beth's mouth. When she didn't protest, he pulled her close and held her for several minutes.

"Now, you were saying?" August asked as he pulled slightly away and lifted Beth's face to meet his stare.

"I don't know what to say," Beth answered.

"Just speak what's on your heart," August urged. He wanted so much to hear Beth say something that would indicate her interest in him.

"That's not always an easy thing to do, August."

"No, maybe not," August said gently stroking Beth's cheek with his thumb. "But it's always the best."

"I'm afraid." Beth's words were barely audible.

"Of me?" August questioned, hurt showing on his face.

"No," Beth replied. "I'm afraid of myself. Afraid of trusting too much, caring too much, needing too much."

"Don't be," August said kissing Beth's hand and holding it close to his heart. "Just tell me what you started to say. Tell me what you want."

"Stay," Beth murmured. "I want you to stay."

six

Days later, Beth sat considering her situation. There was, of course, the constant threat of war hanging over like an ever present storm cloud. Added to this was the continual demands of the roadhouse and the responsibility of raising two boys without a father.

Her sons concerned her most, along with the fact that Beth was finally admitting how much she missed the companionship of a husband.

She hadn't realized how lonely she was until the night August had held her and kissed her. It was hard to admit to loneliness with hundreds of uniformed men and civilians milling up and down the path that ran in front of her roadhouse, but Beth was lonely. August only made that fact more evident.

True to his promise, August had accompanied her and the boys to Sunday school and church. He had appeared aloof and uncomfortable during the worship service, but he said nothing and acted as though he were simply preoccupied. Afterward, they'd enjoyed a wonderful summer afternoon, picnicking, fishing, and simply enjoying each other's company.

It was hard not to think about those moments with August, as well as their first kiss. Beth had made it very clear to August that she wanted him to stay. What she hadn't said was that she needed him to stay; she needed his company and his friendship in a way she couldn't begin to explain.

August had wanted Beth to talk about her feelings, but how could she when she scarcely understood them herself? And what about the issue of why August was avoiding God? There was a great deal about August Eriksson that Beth didn't understand, and those issues were important enough to her so that she wanted to go slow.

Beth pulled out her ledger books and tried to concentrate on the numbers. She made it through one or two lines before her thoughts drifted off. Suddenly, she was a million miles away from balancing the roadhouse books.

August's appearance in her life had brought so many benefits. The relationship he shared with her sons was a precious friendship that filled some of the void their father's death had created.

Phillip and Gerald accepted August as if he'd been JB returning from the war. It didn't matter to them, even after countless explanations, that August wasn't their daddy. Phillip refused to call him anything else, and often Gerald slipped up and referred to him that way. Beth found it increasingly acceptable for her boys to use the title, and when Gerald put JB's picture in the china cupboard, she realized he was symbolizing an end to his need for JB's memory.

Beth couldn't explain why she didn't fight the action or why it seemed perfectly natural to share her meals and spare time with a man she barely knew. But for the first time in months, her boys were happy, and neither one had bad dreams or moped around looking for a man who would never come home.

Looking down at her hand, Beth suddenly realized that she'd nearly twisted her wedding ring off her finger. She stared at the band for a moment, then pulled it off quickly and put it in the desk drawer. JB was gone, and August was here. Perhaps it was time to deal with the matter head on.

Giving up on the ledgers, Beth made her way through the house picking up toys and misplaced items. What a difference one year made! Where once baby rattles and teething rings had dotted the counters, now blocks and trucks sprouted up. Her babies had grown up so fast that it left Beth aching for the feel of holding them close. Perhaps she'd have more children one day.

The thought stunned her. She hadn't considered remarrying until August came into her life, and now she was contemplating a larger family. Maybe August wouldn't want more children.

"Stop it!" Beth said aloud. "I can't think this way. I've got myself married off and having more children, and all to a man I scarcely know!" The empty house absorbed her words, perfectly content to keep her secrets.

Outside, a summer storm was brewing. Beth could hear thunder rumble in the distance. She fought the urge to cry. Things weren't going badly at all, so why did she feel so blue?

The boys were spending the day in town with the woman who led their Sunday school class at the small inter-denominational church. Mrs. Miller was a pleasant woman with graying hair and a grandmotherly shape. Being a widow of several years as well as childless, Mrs. Miller had aligned herself with Beth.

She was particularly fond of Phillip and Gerald, and when the older widow had invited the boys for lunch at her house, Beth had agreed, understanding Mrs. Miller's need. Now, however, Beth reconsidered. The house seemed empty and far too quiet.

Beth sighed. What was wrong with her? She had but to look out her front window and see more activity than most small towns could boast.

The path was being widened to meet road specifications, and Beth could count on no less than twenty different men pounding on her front door daily, seeking everything from water to food to permission to use the privy. She caught on, only after August informed her, that most of the men were doing it to have a chance to talk to the handsome widow of Gantry Roadhouse.

Beth blushed crimson as she remembered August's laughing eyes and boyish grin. He was amused that she had been too naïve to figure it out for herself.

"You're a beautiful woman, Beth Hogan," he had said, "and most of these men haven't had the opportunity to see, much less visit with, a woman of any kind since leaving the States and being assigned to this wilderness. Women are mighty scarce up here, so you might as well get used to being popular."

Beth had feared August would think she'd done something to encourage the attention, but he never spoke of it and never seemed to mind when the boys told stories of visiting strangers.

The highway had been excellent for business, and because of this and the workers' avid interest, Beth could boast a lengthy list of men who were waiting their turn to take residence in her boarding house. Many of these made the excuse of checking on the availability of rooms and stayed on talking of the weather, the highway, or anything else that would delay their return to work.

Yet Beth was still lonely, and she couldn't understand why.

The clock in the hall chimed two, and Beth realized that her cakes were ready to come out of the oven. She had doubled up on baking, knowing that the next day would be devoted to washing clothes and linens, a job that always took an entire day. Often she was still hanging laundry after August arrived home.

Hurrying to the kitchen, Beth pulled out two cake pans along with an experimental recipe she was trying. The sourdough coffee cake, complete with berries and honey, looked every bit as good as it smelled, and Beth was hopeful that its flavor would match its appearance.

Silently, Beth thanked God for the endless supply of honey that one of her bachelor neighbors provided in exchange for mending and sewing. The older man seemed more than happy to give Beth all the honey she could use and even happier to spend time visiting and telling the boys tales of the old days when he'd lived off the land and searched for gold.

Beth realized that because of such generosity and bartering for goods, she and the boys scarcely felt the effects of rationing that the war had made necessary. God had been truly good to them.

When her baking was completed, Beth was amazed to realize she still had almost two hours to pass before the boys and August would be home. August had agreed to pick the boys up at Mrs. Miller's house in order to spare either of the ladies from making the trip. At the time, Beth couldn't find any reason not to accept his offer. Now she wished she had a reason to take the long stroll into town.

Heaving a sigh, Beth decided to stop feeling sorry for herself. Instead, she would cook a special meal for her family's return. Putting her hands to work usually occupied her mind as well. Hopefully working on dinner would make the afternoon pass more quickly.

She thoughtfully chose foods that she knew everyone was fond of. Smoked salmon would be their meat, and for a side dish, Beth blended new potatoes, fresh green beans, and pieces of side meat. For dessert, they'd try her new berry coffee cake, a sure way, Beth decided, to know whether or not it was acceptable.

She was just finishing the table setting, using her finest tablecloth and wedding china, when she heard the boys' non-stop chatter as they drew near home. *What a beautiful sound,* Beth thought. She was so used to the constant noise of the road construction that when the men had stopped for supper, Beth hadn't noticed.

She was grateful that the army was taking time away from the project to have their own evening meal. No doubt with the added hours of light there'd soon be another shift at work, but for now Beth was going to thoroughly enjoy the noise that her sons raised and the words that August Eriksson would share at her dinner table.

"Mommy!" Gerald hollered as he came through the door. August followed with Phillip on his shoulders.

Beth smiled and welcomed Gerald into her arms. "Did you have a good time at Mrs. Miller's house?"

"Uh-huh," Gerald said and held up a small sack. "We made cookies, and Mrs. Miller said we could bring them home."

"How nice of her," Beth said and turned her attention from Gerald to Phillip. "And how about you, buster? Did you have a good time?"

"I had fun," Phillip answered. "I got to ride up here on Daddy's shoulders all the way home."

"And I believe this child is eating too much," August said as he lifted Phillip over his head and placed him on the ground. "Well, well. What's all this?" he said as he noticed the table.

"I just thought something special might be nice," Beth answered. "I had so much time on my hands with the boys gone. I never knew a body could get so lonely."

August offered a tender smile, and Beth quickly turned her face away to avoid feeling the impact of his clear eyes. "You boys, go wash your hands and we'll sit down to dinner."

Handing his mother the cookies, Gerald scurried off to the washroom with Phillip close behind. Both boys were giggling and chattering all the way, leaving Beth with a much lighter heart.

"I'm sorry if I made you uncomfortable," August said as he paused before following the boys. "I just don't like to think of you lonely. Seems like such a waste, especially when so many enjoy your company."

Beth wondered if it was her imagination or August's feelings that caused her to read more into his statement.

When August and the boys returned from washing up, Beth allowed August to seat her while the boys scampered into their assigned places.

"Who wants to say grace?" Beth questioned.

"I will!" Gerald said enthusiastically.

"All right, Gerald," Beth nodded in agreement. "You go right ahead."

"God, this is Gerald again," the boy began. "I sure do like living in Alaska 'cause You sent us a lot of great people and we're having fun here. God, Mommy told me to pray about a daddy for Phillip and me, so I'm praying about it. I like August, God, and I really want him to be my daddy. So if it's okay with You, me and Phillip will take him. Amen."

"What about the food, son?" August questioned softly noticing that Beth's head was still bowed.

"Oh yeah," Gerald said and quickly bowed his head again. "Thanks for the food, God. I really like fish. Amen."

August was grinning when Beth raised her gaze to meet his. She grew more beautiful with each passing day, and August heartily agreed with Gerald's prayers that they become a family.

Beth handed Phillip's plate to August. "If you would serve the salmon," she motioned, "I would appreciate it."

August nodded and filled the plates as they were passed to him. He liked acting as the head of the family, and he enjoyed the warmth and comfort of the company he kept.

Supper passed much too quickly. "I suppose I should be going," August said, getting up. Beth's roadhouse was set up so that the ten boarding rooms all faced north or west and had individual entrances facing the outside.

"Can't he read us a story?" Gerald asked with pleading eyes.

"Please?" Phillip questioned.

"That's up to August," Beth said as she began to gather the dishes. "It's all right with me, August, if you want to read to them."

"I'd be happy to," August said, grateful for the excuse to remain close at hand. He followed the boys down the hall to their bedroom, giving Beth a quick smile over his shoulder.

Beth felt her pulse quicken. What would it be like to have August join her for the evening every night after putting their children to bed? It had been so long since she'd known the warmth and comfort of a man's company. Was it wrong for her to think of such things?

"Well, that didn't take long," August said as he came into the kitchen. "They're nearly asleep."

"Thank you for everything," Beth said and tried to think of how she could express her gratitude for August's indulgence of their fatherly references. "I appreciate your patience with them. I've asked them not to call you Daddy," she paused, embarrassed as she remembered Gerald's prayer. "But they love you so much."

"I'm sure that they loved their father a great deal. They're just showing me what they can't show him."

"It's more than that. JB was a soldier first. He was so bent on serving his country and being a hero," Beth said as she finished drying the dishes. She didn't see August bite his lip at her words.

"Don't get me wrong," she said, turning to face him. "JB was a good man and a fine father. He loved children and we were planning to have a half a dozen or more, but his need to serve someone else or something else took him away from us. I don't blame him or resent him for his decision, but I don't think I'll ever understand the feelings that drive a man to leave his family and die a world away from those who love him."

"It's a powerful drive indeed," August said softly. "I'm sure JB felt proud, and in his heart he knew that he was offering his children the best he had. He gave his life that others might live free."

"Much like Christ gave His life for us," Beth said, startling August.

"I suppose that's true," he agreed. "If Christ felt it necessary to come on our behalf and give His life, then maybe you can understand JB's desire to offer what he could for those he loved."

"Maybe you're right," Beth said as she considered August's words. "Jesus certainly loves us more than we can comprehend."

August looked uncomfortable, so Beth decided to say no more. "I'd better go," August finally said. "I'll have to be up pretty early, so don't worry about breakfast. I'll get something in town."

"All right," Beth said and watched as August walked quietly from the house. She whispered a prayer that August would find a way through whatever problem was causing him to feel alienated from God's peace.

August made his way to his room. Even though it

was still light outside and would be for many hours, August closed the heavy shutters and prepared for bed. It was warm enough that he wouldn't need to light the stove.

He lay awake for a long time thinking about the things Beth had said and how she constantly tried to steer him back to God. His conscience bothered him as he thought of the truth that he continued to deny.

God clearly wanted his attention, but August wasn't inclined to let go of his bitterness. God still hadn't listened to the desires of August's heart, and because of that, August questioned what purpose faith served.

As he drifted into a fitful sleep, August remembered how his inability to get into the army brought him to both his important job with the highway and Beth Hogan. One door had closed while another had opened and shown him a new way of life. But where did God fit in?

seven

With the boys busy playing in the backyard treehouse, Beth took a moment out of her morning chores
to enjoy a hot cup of coffee and a letter from her
friend, Karen Sawin.

Karen shared bits of information, including the
news that her husband had suffered an injury and
was being sent home. Beth wished she could be there
to help her friend, but travel was nearly impossible
because of the war.

Reading on, Beth was glad to learn that the family
who'd purchased her home was being blessed with
yet another child and had plans to build onto the house
in order to accommodate the addition.

Finishing the letter, Beth noted the fear and apprehension that Karen expressed as she awaited her
husband's return. Beth whispered a prayer for her
friend as she refolded the paper.

Setting the letter aside, Beth picked up a pad and
pencil and scratched out a reminder to write to Karen
at the first possible moment. She knew Karen would
need all the encouragement she could get.

Beth glanced out the window to make certain the
boys hadn't fallen out of the tree. She had faced the
treehouse with fear, but August had convinced her
that boys needed such things. Who was she to argue
with his wisdom? Giggles filtered down, assuring
Beth that nothing was amiss.

Back at the table, Beth sipped weak coffee and tried to plan out the rest of the day. She jotted notes about lunch and supper, but inevitably her mind returned to thoughts of August. She could picture him standing in the yard playing with her children or chopping wood. He was an appealing man with a handsome face and a gentleness that she'd rarely seen in others. Her feelings for him were growing, but she knew he was troubled about God.

What was it that had hurt August so much that he couldn't deal with God? Beth contemplated that question as she continued to enjoy the quiet.

"Beth?" August called from the front room.

Beth glanced at her watch and then at the clock on the wall. It was only nine o'clock. What was August doing back at this hour?

"In here," Beth called and got to her feet. August came through the kitchen door with a worried look on his face. "What is it?" Beth questioned, knowing that August had something to tell her.

"You'd better sit down," August said and pulled the chair out for Beth.

"What is it?" Beth repeated the question.

"What I'm going to tell you has to be kept secret, at least until you read about it in the newspapers."

"I don't understand," Beth said and felt her stomach knot.

"You know why the highway was planned, don't you?"

"Sure," Beth replied. "The government felt it was important to have an emergency road in order to get supplies through."

"That's right," August said. "Well, now we may

very well need the road."

"Why?" Beth questioned. "What's happened?"

"This is the part you mustn't tell anyone. The army took us into their confidence this morning. The Japanese have attacked the Aleutian Islands," August announced.

"The Aleutians? But that's less than six hundred miles away," Beth said as the color drained from her face. "Dear Lord, preserve us."

"Look, Beth, the Aleutians are a long ways off. We're safe here, but the road project has been stepped up. We've got work to do and not much time to do it in. The troops are holding the Japanese back, but it's critical we get this road through."

Tears filled Beth's eyes. "Are we really safe? I mean, are you sure?"

August saw the tears and heard Beth's voice tremble. He got up and put his hands on her shoulders just as she broke down.

"I can't bear it, August. I can't stand the fear, the worry. I have children whose safety depends on me. I just can't bear the thought of the enemy storming in here and, and. . ." Beth's sobs filled the air.

"Don't torture yourself, Beth. We really are safe. After all, there are more than ten thousand soldiers in Alaska and Canada. There's more than enough manpower here to keep us safe."

Beth pushed away from August and got to her feet. "We probably had thousands of men in the Pacific as well. If men are so capable, why are we at war?"

"We're at war because we have to fight to keep free of dictators like Hitler and Mussolini, as well as military monsters like Tojo. Beth, please don't cry.

Everything will work out. You'll see. Just have a little faith."

Beth managed to compose herself. "Yes, of course you're right, August. Faith is the key. Faith in God, though, not in the American military. God will give them strength and wisdom. Prayer is going to be the key to this victory, and I'm sorry that I let go of that wisdom."

August stepped forward and put his hand on Beth's arm. "I just wanted you to know what was going on before you heard about it from someone else. No doubt the newspaper will have enough about it in the days to come, but I never wanted to upset you. I know news like this can be frightening."

"I'm all right now," Beth said as she lifted her apron and dried her eyes. She wanted so much to prove her faith to August. Perhaps he'd once had faith, too, a faith that he'd lost because of tragedy. Maybe this was the reason God had sent August Eriksson into her life—not for love or marriage, but for him to see the truth of God's love.

August studied her for a moment. He wanted to hold her, to make her believe that everything would be all right, but in spite of the feelings that continued to grow, August held himself back.

There was something in Beth's eyes that signaled aloofness. She was content to put the entire matter in God's hands, and it seemed to August that she didn't need or desire his comfort. Shrugging his shoulders, he left the roadhouse with an ache in his heart for something he couldn't explain.

The hot June sun caused sweat to pour down August's

back as he maneuvered the caterpillar into position. He was frustrated by Beth's attitude and wondered how he could combat it. She never came out and talked with him about her true feelings. She always managed to hide behind God or biblical principles, almost as if she knew it would distance Augusthim.

Wiping his forehead with the back of his hand, August acknowledged that his biggest problem wasn't Beth. God was pricking his conscience.

It was the little things that got to him. Things like the way Beth would ask him to say grace or the way Gerald would talk about something from Sunday school. Sometimes it was the simple, quiet moments when August was alone in his room and the silence came over him as if roaring out God's name.

He'd not known a single moment's peace since turning away from his heavenly Father, and the turmoil within his heart only grew. August wanted to shout out for God to leave him alone, but the pressure continued, mounting day by day.

The road work took August away from Beth and the boys for longer periods of time. Sometimes he never made it home because the midnight sun allowed them to work nearly around the clock. Often, August would drop exhausted into a sleeping bag inside one of the administration's tents. The cots weren't nearly as comfortable as the bed back at the roadhouse, but as tired as he was, it wouldn't have mattered if he'd been sleeping on the ground.

Day after day the work continued. They called it "bulldozer surveying," and it was little more than plowing a path through a place where a road had never been intended. Trees, brush, and rock ended up in messy piles along the road, constant reminders of the haste in which the design was completed.

August would often stare for a long time at the tall spruce and birch trees, trees so thick and full that they were impossible to penetrate with the human eye. It seemed a pity to destroy them.

Dense forests were relieved by brilliant, crystal lakes so blue and inviting that August could almost forget his purpose. Glacier-fed rivers flowed in milky wonder, leaving reminders of the ice mountains which had carved the valleys.

In the distant south, snow-capped peaks rose majestically above green and blue valleys, and everywhere, wildflowers carpeted the earth in colors so dazzling and radiant that words could not describe them.

"Eriksson!" a voice called above the roar of the cat's engine. August shut the motor off and climbed down.

"What's up, Bill?" August questioned, recognizing the man beneath layers of dirt and sweat.

"I'm supposed to take over your shift. Supervisor wants to see you."

"Oh?" He wondered about the request as he went in search of Ralph Greening.

Ralph was waiting for August in his tent. "Come on in," Ralph waved him in as he finished up a radio call. "Sorry for the interruption, but I have some good news for you."

"Well, I'm always in the mood for good news interruptions," August said with a smile.

"You've done a tremendous job for us, August, and I'd like to offer you a permanent position with the Public Roads Administration. You'd actually be left in charge of the Northway area after we pull out. They are going to want to establish a permanent road next year, and I can't think of a better man to leave behind."

"I'm flattered," August said.

"Well, you've certainly earned it," Ralph replied as he shuffled through a stack of papers. "I'll be happy to return to the States and get away from these monstrous bugs and all this light. A body needs regular nights and days. I can't figure out how you folks put up with constant light and then endless darkness."

"I guess when you're born here you don't give it a lot of thought. We do suffer in the winter, though. It's hard to wake up in the dark, spend the day in the dark, and then go to sleep in the dark. Coupled with the cold—and I mean bitter, sub-zero cold—it is a problem," August replied. "But there are winter compensations."

"I don't intend to be here long enough to find out. We plan to have the road completed before then, and after that you can put up with it."

Hours later, August contemplated his promotion and the full responsibility that would be his when Ralph returned to the States. Did he want to head up such a task?

As he settled down for bed, August wondered at the turn of events. Not long ago he'd thought God had deserted him. How did he feel now? Hadn't he proved to himself that he could live life without God?

He missed Beth and the boys. It had been over a week since he'd seen them. They were so important to him, and thoughts of them were never far from his mind. Did they ever think of him? Did they miss him like he missed them?

August closed his eyes, envisioning Bethany as she moved around her roadhouse. She was so gentle and pure, and her heart was devoted to God.

His heart had once belonged to God, too. August shifted uncomfortably as he thought of his efforts to put God away from him. *But whosoever shall deny me before men, him will I also deny before my Father which is in heaven.* August remembered the words of Matthew 10:33 almost against his will.

"But you took away all my dreams, God," August argued, realizing that for the first time in months, he was speaking to God. "You took it all: my dreams, my hopes, my family. Am I to be forsaken because I dared to think for myself, dared to make goals and dream dreams? I thought you wanted Your children to be happy. Am I to give up my dreams, even my very life, in order to be at peace with You?"

He that findeth his life shall lose it: and he that loseth his life for my sake shall find it. August pulled the pillow over his head as if he could block out the haunting words of Matthew 10:39. The words, however, would not be put aside. God's Word had made its home in August's heart for many years, and it would not leave just because August wished to escape its power.

eight

After spending two weeks without August in their home, Beth, Gerald, and Phillip were excited to see his weary frame coming up the path late one afternoon.

"Daddy!" Phillip announced when he spotted August. "Momma, Daddy's here!"

Beth glanced out the window, and her hands automatically smoothed back her blond hair. August was home!

Gerald went dancing out the door, rushing to August's arms. "I missed you," he said as August whirled him around.

"And I missed you! Have you been a good boy?"

"I've been very helpful, just like you told me to be," Gerald said as August put him down.

Phillip hurried to be next in August's arms, while Beth stood to the side of the door, wishing she had the freedom her children enjoyed.

August's eyes met hers over Phillip's back. He noticed the softness and grinned at her, causing Beth's heart to pound harder.

"And what about you?" Beth heard August ask Phillip. "Have you been a good boy?"

"Uh-huh. I been helping in the garden," Phillip said, holding up his dirty hands. "See!"

His enthusiasm was contagious. "Yes, I see." August said, inspecting Phillip's hands. "Since you've

both been so good, I'll take you fishing tomorrow.
That is if your mother doesn't mind."

"Can we go, Momma?" Phillip and Gerald asked
in unison.

"I suppose so," Beth replied softly. "Now why
don't you go inside and get cleaned up? It's almost
supper time."

The boys hesitated as they looked from August to
their mother and back again. "You go ahead, boys.
I'll be here for a day or two." At August's reassurance the boys disappeared into the house.

"I've missed you," August said warmly. "I never
knew how good I had it until I had to live out on the
road. I've missed everything about this place."

"Even the bugs?" Beth asked with a smile.

"The bugs are even bigger down the road. Out there
we have to shoot them down rather than swat them."
August laughed and Beth joined him. When the
amusement passed, silence bound them together.

"You look beautiful." August braved the words and
allowed his eyes to travel Beth's form. The dusty rose
dress she wore brought out the flush in her cheeks.

Beth didn't know what to say. She was excited by
August's appreciation of her appearance, yet she was
troubled by the warning her mind kept flashing.

"Are you hungry?" she finally questioned, growing uncomfortable in the silence.

"Yes," August replied. "I suppose I'm keeping you
from something."

"Only dinner," Beth answered and opened the
screen door. "Come on inside. I'll work while you
tell me about the road's progress."

"It's a deal," August said, following Beth into the

house and on to the kitchen.

"I took a moose roast out of the freezer several days ago, and we've been eating on it ever since," Beth said as she opened the oven door. "We're having moose pie tonight."

"Moose pie?"

Beth smiled as she took the casserole from the oven. "That's right. It's moose roast cut up with eggplant, onions, egg, cheese, and seasoning. It's baked with a pie-crust topping, and that's why we call it moose pie."

"Sounds good," August said, sitting down.

"I can fix up a mess of goosetongue greens, if you've a mind for a salad, and I have fresh sourdough bread."

"Don't go to any more trouble than you already have," August said.

Before Beth could answer, a knock sounded at the front door. "I'll be right back," Beth said as she excused herself.

"What a surprise," Beth said as she opened the door to Mrs. Miller. Ushering the woman inside, she asked, "What brings you here?"

"I know it's last minute and totally out of line, but I was wondering if I could borrow the boys to help me gather blackberries. I've promised the army a great deal of jam, and there's a huge field of berries ready to pick."

"Well, I'm not sure," Beth said as she led the way back to the kitchen. "Mr. Eriksson is back, and the boys are very fond of him. I don't know if we could separate them just now."

"I understand, but I could sure use the help. I'd be

happy to pay the boys," the older woman added as she struggled to keep up with Beth.

"Oh no, you needn't pay them," Beth said as they entered the kitchen. In her absence, the boys had been taking turns playing with August and asking him questions.

"Boys, Mrs. Miller wants to know if you can help her pick blackberries."

"But August just got here," Gerald protested from August's lap.

"And I'll be here for a while," August said and gave Gerald a reassuring pat. "Don't worry about it. You go ahead and help Mrs. Miller. We can certainly catch up on our talking tomorrow while we're fishing."

"Well, I guess we can help," Gerald said once he felt certain of August's presence.

"I'm afraid the boys haven't eaten yet, Mrs. Miller. Would you like to join us for supper?" Beth asked, proud that Gerald had put his own wants aside to help someone else.

"No thanks, and if you don't mind, I'd like to treat the boys to a picnic. I have sandwiches and cold drinks, as well as some special cookies that they are very fond of," Mrs. Miller answered.

"Well, what do you say, boys? You want to have a picnic with Mrs. Miller?" August questioned before Beth could ask. "I'll bet it'll be a load of fun."

"Really, Daddy?" Phillip asked with wide eyes.

"Why sure. It's a beautiful evening, and Mrs. Miller makes mighty good cookies. I know 'cause she brought us some while we were working on the air-strip."

"Okay," Gerald said as he hopped down from August's lap. "We'll go."

"I'm really grateful, boys," Mrs. Miller said, motioning toward the door. "Let's hurry so we can eat before we pick the berries."

The boys went along with Mrs. Miller, and Beth was left to face August alone.

"I guess we'll have more than enough supper," Beth said as she finished putting the food on the table. She took a seat across from August and realized it was the first time they'd shared dinner alone. Always before they'd had the comfort of the boys to dispel any tension, but now they sat face to face, both seeming to know they were going to deal with more than supper.

"I'll say grace," Beth said avoiding August's eyes. She bowed her head without waiting to see if August would and began, "Dear Father, we thank You for this meal and the fellowship we share. Bless us now and guard us in our steps. Amen."

August held out his hand for Beth's plate, dished out a generous portion of the steaming casserole, and handed it back to her.

"Thank you," Beth said. She wanted to say so much more, yet she felt a sense of quiet come over her, as if it were more important that August begin the conversation.

"This is real good," August said with a nod of approval. "I've had moose steak, moose roast, moose stew, but I don't think I've ever had moose pie. I'll have to send my sister the recipe."

"I'm glad you like it," Beth replied between bites. Food stuck in her throat, and she remembered she hadn't set out any beverage. "I'll get us something to drink. What would you like?"

"It doesn't much matter to me. Whatever you had planned is fine," August answered.

"I have some powdered lemonade that one of the soldiers traded me for pies. I fixed a batch this morning, and it ought to be good and cold by now."

"That sounds good."

Beth smiled and went to fix the glasses and juice. Once this was accomplished, she sat back down to face the unnerving silence.

"I think the boys have grown a foot taller," August said as he ate.

"Yes," Beth replied. "I'm going to have to get them new mukluks this fall."

"Say, I saw some dandy native-made ones just down the road. There's a small village not far from where the highway is going through, and a bunch of us went over to check out the situation and found a wealth of hand-made goods."

"It would certainly be great to buy something without worrying about ration stamps. Is it too far to walk?" Beth questioned.

"I wouldn't think so," August said, trying to remember the exact distance. "But maybe you could get someone to run you over, just to be on the safe side. I'll talk to Ralph and see if I can borrow one of the vehicles and drive you there myself."

"Oh, I wouldn't want to take you away from your work," Beth replied.

"It wouldn't take me away from anything," August insisted. "I've been given a couple days off due to the long hours I've been putting in. I'll see what I can do and let you know."

"All right," she reluctantly agreed.

The silence returned to hang between them like an impenetrable veil. Even August shifted uncomfortably and nervously picked at his food. Finally, he put his fork down, folded his hands, and eased back against his chair.

"I have something to say," he began.

"I thought you might," Beth answered and put her own fork down.

August gazed across the table, allowing himself several moments to take in the vision of Beth's beauty. Beth's pale blond hair was pulled back from her face, revealing high cheekbones and soft white skin. Her blue eyes seemed to grow larger under August's stare.

"I don't know all the sweet words or wily ways that men work with women, but what I have to say comes from the heart. While I've been gone I've done a lot of thinking."

"I see," Beth murmured.

"No, I don't think you do," August said softly. "I mostly thought of you. And of course, the boys." August waited for Beth to make some reply, but she only lowered her eyes.

"I guess I came to realize how important you were to me. I found myself thinking of you and how wonderful you felt in my arms. I thought of the boys and how they always treat me like their father—how Phillip even calls me Daddy. And I had to explain to you."

"Explain what?" Beth asked.

"I love you, Beth. I think I've loved you for a long time, but since I've never been in love, I just didn't recognize it. I knew you were special to me and the boys were always great, but it wasn't until I had to spend a long time away from you, from all of you, that I realized how important you were to me."

"What exactly do you mean?"

"I want to marry you, Beth. I know you're still mourning JB's passing, but I can wait for you. I want to help you make a new life, and I want to be a father to your children and to have more children, together."

Beth wasn't surprised at August's declaration, but neither was she prepared for the proposal. Shadows fell across the room as the sun continued its journey west, and Beth got up to turn on the lights.

August waited impatiently for her to say something, anything that might let him know how she felt. He watched Beth come back to the table and stand behind her chair.

"When I learned that JB was joining the air force, something inside me came undone. Phillip was just a baby, and Gerald wasn't much out of diapers. I cried when JB told me that he would have to go away and that once his training was completed, he'd be sent to Europe immediately. He told me it might be years before we saw each other again, and a part of me died." Beth drew a deep breath before continuing.

"JB had such a love of life and of God, and I knew that I couldn't make him stay. Truly, I didn't want to impose my will upon him, but in my heart I knew he'd never come home again. Of course, I never told JB that. I prayed about it, pouring out my heart before God, and I sought the Scriptures, hoping and praying to find something sensible to ease my worries.

"'Trust in the Lord with all thine heart; and lean not unto thine own understanding.' That's Proverbs 3:5," Beth said.

"Yes, I know," August replied with a nod. "Go on."

"Well, that was the verse God led me to. I kept wanting to trust my own understanding about things. I reasoned that I had it all figured out. After all, God had sent me a wonderful Christian husband and two beautiful sons. I didn't have any reason to believe that all wouldn't be well, but in my heart I had a gnawing fear that wouldn't pass. When I received notice that JB was dead and knew that my fears were fulfilled, I almost felt relieved. Does that sound strange?"

"Not really," August said and added, "everyone deals with things the best way they can. You were anticipating the worst and the waiting is always the hardest part. When the worst that could happen finally happened, you were able to relax, knowing that things were as bad as they were going to get."

"I suppose that's true," Beth said as she gripped the chair back. "I turned my heart and soul to God for comfort. There was nothing else to do and no one else to pull me through. Do you understand?" August nodded. "I hold my relationship with Him quite dear. He pulled me through losing JB and kept me sane so that my children didn't suffer from the loss."

"Why are you telling me all this? I already know that you still mourn JB. I wouldn't intrude on that. I only ask to remain close at hand until those feelings pass."

"That's what I'm trying to say," Beth said softly.

"I've already buried the past and JB. He was an important part of my life, but he's in heaven now. I don't have to worry about JB anymore. I miss him, occasionally, but those times come rarely anymore. I've been able to get on with my life, and JB's death is no longer an issue with me. But my love of God and His Word are."

"I don't understand."

"You have an obvious problem when it comes to fellowship with the Lord. Forgive me if that sounds judgmental, but even Gerald knows that you are alienated from God. He's come to me before and asked me why you never pray and why you never talk of God the way I do or the way JB did. He was so tiny when JB went away, but he remembers his father telling him about heaven and God. Proverbs 20:11 says, 'Even a child is known by his doings, whether his work be pure, and whether it be right.' It's obvious to those around you that things are not right." Beth saw a shadow of denial pass through August's eyes.

"I'd love for you to talk to me about what has hurt you and turned you from God. I'd love to be able to help you through your anger and frustration, but you won't let me. You turn away at every possible opportunity."

"Talking won't resolve anything," August stated firmly.

"And marriage will?"

"I love you, Beth!" August said as he pounded his fist against the table.

"And I love you, August," Beth whispered, ignoring the outburst. "But I can't marry you when your heart isn't right with God. It would always stand between us and eventually divide us. I can't serve two masters, and I won't give up God."

"The verse about two masters referred to money," August said stiffly, remembering Luke 16:13.

"The verse says, 'No servant can serve two masters: for either he will hate the one, and love the other; or else he will hold to the one, and despise the other. Ye cannot serve God and mammon.' I think it works in this situation as well," Beth said with a gentle tone.

"I can't hold fast to raising my sons as Christians who will respect the Word and fellowship with believers, when their father denies the need. I can't love you and serve you properly as your wife, and hold onto my faith and serve God as well. Sooner or later, the two will clash, and the battleground will be our home. Would you really have the lives claimed be those of your adopted sons and wife?"

August stared in silence. Beth had forced him to face the one thing he'd refused to admit for so long. How could he explain to her that he'd faced such disappointment that he was no longer certain that he wanted God's will?

"Look," Beth continued, feeling suddenly strengthened, "God has a purpose in all of this, and I believe He has sent us to one another for a special reason. Maybe it's to help each of us deal with the past and the sorrows we've faced. Maybe not. But I know that this problem must be dealt with before we can marry. Do you understand?"

"I don't know," August said as he folded his arms against his chest. "I just don't know. It's all well and fine to use this as a reason to turn me away, but are you sure there isn't something more. You said you love me, was that true?"

"Yes," Beth nodded. "I love you very much."

"Then why not trust God to work everything out after we're married?"

"Because we're both old enough to know it doesn't work that way. August, I would love to marry you. Believe me, I don't like being alone, and I hate the fact that my boys have you only as a friend and not their father. I want us to be a family as much as you do, but I want us to be a family under the hand of God. If we married now, that wouldn't be the case, would it?"

August's dark eyes narrowed, and he clenched his jaw tightly. "If that's the way you want it, then I'll leave. I'm sorry I'm not good enough for you and your children."

August turned on his heel and stormed through the house. Beth followed after him, wishing she could say something that would stop him from leaving her in anger. "I love you, August," she whispered as he opened the screen door.

"But not enough," August replied. He slammed the door behind him and stalked down the drive.

Tears streamed down Beth's face as she watched the man she loved walk out of her life. "It's not enough without God, August," she whispered. "It would never be enough without Him."

nine

August faced each new day with bitterness and trepidation. The highway project kept his hands busy, but his mind continued to be haunted by images of the woman he'd left behind.

He was angry with Beth and with God, but mostly with himself. He knew he'd disappointed Gerald and Phillip by leaving without a word, especially after promising them such a grand day of fishing and story telling. It grieved him that he was causing them pain. Why did life have to be so difficult?

From time to time, as news trickled in about the progress of the war, August felt his anger rekindled. He should have been one of the troops. If only God would have worked things out for him and heard his prayers. If only God cared.

Every day, August operated machinery, issued orders, and helped to assess progress. While he knew the job demanded his undivided attention, his mind incessantly wandered.

Log bridges were built to cross the multiple rivers and creeks, but the problem of boggy, wet ground made process slow and uncertain. River banks had to be reinforced to hold the bridges, and while gravel was readily available, the waterlogged land seemed to have an insatiable appetite. Load after load of rock was brought in to stabilize that which refused to be stable.

Danger lurked behind every tree, and each new and unexplored position placed the highway crew in jeopardy. Despite difficulty and hardship, the highway was steadily becoming reality. August wondered what he would do when the road work was completed.

Ralph Greening expected him to stay on and work for the Public Roads Administration. There were plans to make continued road improvements and to see to it that eventually the Alaskan/Canadian Military Highway would be more than a mud trail through the wilderness. But even for the promise of a secure job, August didn't know if he could live close to Beth and the boys and not be part of their lives.

August tried to put such thoughts from his mind as he joined his crew. Rains had slowed progress, and after a two-day dry spell, every man available was out on the road making up time. Testing the ground, August grimaced. It remained spongy from the deluge, and such conditions only added to the danger of the situation.

August climbed aboard a Caterpillar tractor and started his shift with great reluctance. His duties seemed meaningless, and his life once again held no purpose. But there were tree stumps to be removed and the road to be graded.

Paying little attention to the twenty-ton machine he maneuvered, August wasn't aware of how precariously close he had come to the edge of a sheer drop. His mind was too preoccupied to notice the ledge giving way, and by the time he recognized the danger, it was too late. In a mass of rubble and a cloud of diesel smoke, the machine slid down the embankment. All August could do was hold on.

It seemed an eternity of bouncing, pitching, and turning. Then the tractor came to rest on its side, pinning August beneath.

August felt the warmth of his own blood as it gushed from a cut above his left eye. He tried to assess the situation, but his mind was clouded and dull, and his eyes refused to stay open. He struggled to move his arms, but any movement was impossible.

I have to get out of this, August thought. He strained against the weight which pinned him firmly against the ground. He could feel cold, boggy dampness against his back, and he tried to remember if a lake or pond sat near where he'd been grading. His mind offered only hazy memories.

He heard voices overhead and knew his men would come to his aid. It was hard to figure out just where they were and how soon he could expect relief, but just hearing them gave him comfort.

"Why is this happening, God?" August wondered aloud. "Why must I suffer these torments and pains?" As it became a monumental effort just to breathe, August fell silent.

Minutes or maybe hours passed as August faded in and out of consciousness. He thought he heard people working overhead, but the roar in his head made it impossible to know for certain.

"August. August," a voice called out, and though he couldn't see the face, August answered.

"I'm here! I'm under here!"

"I know where you are. August, do you trust me to get you out?"

What a strange question, August thought. *Why*

would anyone ask me that?

"I don't know who you are," August replied, "but if you can help to get me out of here, I'd be much obliged."

"August, do you believe in me?" The voice whispered.

August shook his head. "What are you talking about? Just get me out of this. I'll believe you, shake your hand, dance a jig, whatever you want. Just get me out from under this thing!"

August knew his words sounded harsh and ungrateful, but this man was beginning to bother him.

"August, you called upon me. Dost thou believe on the Son of God?"

A tingle ran down August's spine. Those words were Scripture. He remembered them very well. Jesus had asked that question of a blind man.

August's breath quickened. What was it that the man answered in the Bible? August thought for a moment before quoting John 9:36 in a hesitant voice. "'Who is he, Lord, that I might believe on him?'"

"Thou hast both seen him, and it is he that talketh with thee." The words paralleled Christ's reply in the Bible.

August felt a trembling that started in his toes and worked all the way up through his body. The love of a Savior whom he'd so long denied penetrated the darkness and cold that engulfed his body.

Suddenly all the bitterness melted away from August's heart. In an instant, the blindness of his anger lifted, and he could once again see. He remembered the closeness and comfort that came from being right with God.

"I've really made a mess of things, Lord. Forgive me," August cried out. "Please forgive me."

August wept tears of repentance as he thought of God's love. Even though he'd rejected that love, Jesus had reached through the wall of August's disappointment and denial to be at his side when August needed Him most. What a precious friend!

The presence of Christ at his side never subsided, even as the tractor was lifted from overhead. August struggled to open his eyes, but they felt heavy and weighted down.

"August, August, old buddy, wake up. Wake up!" one of the men called.

August opened his eyes to see the hazy image of several men. Above them the spruce trees parted to reveal a brilliant sky of cobalt blue. August tried to sit up, but firm hands held him down.

"Don't move, August. You're hurt pretty bad. We're going to get you some help. Just hang on."

August tried to remain conscious, but his mind flooded with blackness, and his body went limp.

"Maybe it's better this way," one worker said to another. "I wouldn't want to be awake when they moved me. Not with the way his body must be broken up inside." The men agreed as they waited for a stretcher.

Coming out of the darkness was much like surfacing after diving deep into a lake. Fighting against the urge to remain in the dark stillness, August awoke to strange voices and blinding pain. Feeling as though every part of his body was broken, August moaned in agony.

"He's awake, Doctor," a young woman's voice called.

A man peered down at August with a look of concern. "Mr. Eriksson, I'm Dr. Butler. Can you understand me?"

"Yes," August answered slowly. Even speaking seemed painful.

"Mr. Eriksson, you've sustained some injuries. We won't know the extent of those injuries until our examination is complete. You have a concussion and a deep laceration on your forehead. Other than that, it's hard to tell. We'll do what we can to make you comfortable."

"Where am I?" August asked, knowing that there hadn't been any hospitals in the area where he had been working.

"Anchorage. They flew you in yesterday."

"I've been unconscious that long?"

"I'm afraid so, but don't worry. It isn't at all unusual after sustaining a severe head injury. For now, I'd just like you to rest and let us do our job."

August gave a slight nod before drifting into a deep, peaceful sleep.

Three days later, August was propped up in bed, trying to absorb a full assessment of his condition.

"You are most fortunate, Mr. Eriksson," the doctor explained. "Had you landed on a hard surface, you'd most likely be dead. Instead, you landed in wet muskeg which caused your body to sink beneath the weight of the tractor. When they were able to pull the machinery from you, they discovered that you were beneath the ground's surface. No one can explain why the tractor didn't sink right along with you, but perhaps the weight was better distributed. There's really no way of knowing," the doctor said as he glanced back and forth from August's face to the chart he held.

"Some might, in fact, call it a miracle. It took over four hours to free you, and you were unconscious the entire time. Fortunately, you didn't lose much blood," Dr. Butler added.

"But I remember being awake. I remember talking to. . ." August's voice fell silent.

"I can only go by what the pilot passed on to me from the road crew. However, it would fit with the nature of your injuries. Besides the concussion, you have a broken collar bone on the left side and some relatively minor lacerations elsewhere. We were fearful that you might have sustained several fractured lumbar vertebrae."

"Several what?" August questioned. Although his sister was a registered nurse, he had never taken the time to learn much more than the basics that kept him alive.

"We thought your back might be broken, but it appears that all is well. I'd say several weeks will right what's wrong, and you'll be able to return to your home. I strongly caution against any strenuous labor, however, for at least two or three months."

"That long?" August asked in a weary voice.

"I'm sorry, Mr. Eriksson," the doctor sympathized, "but as I've already stated, you're lucky to be alive."

"Not lucky," August said with a weak grin. "God saved me from death, and believe me, I'm grateful."

"Well then, I expect a good patient who's obedient

to orders," Dr. Butler answered and turned to leave. "And I happen to agree with you, Mr. Eriksson. You were very blessed."

August nodded and relaxed as the doctor left. No sooner had he walked through the door then a gray-haired nurse entered the room.

"Good day, Mr. Eriksson," the pleasant-voiced woman said. "I'm Nurse Roberts. How are you feeling?"

"Well enough, I suppose."

"Good, good. I'll need to take your temperature and pulse now," the woman said as she automatically popped a thermometer in August's mouth and took his wrist.

The woman reminded August of his mother. She was firm, yet gentle in her touch, and her voice was like a spoken lullaby.

"I'll bet you'd enjoy some breakfast," she chattered after marking down his pulse rate. "Well, I have just the thing for you. Eggs, toast, juice, and maybe even some bacon. How about it?" she questioned, removing the thermometer from August's mouth.

"It sounds wonderful," August agreed.

"Then I'll fetch you a tray and be back in a jiffy," Nurse Roberts announced and hurried from the room.

August contemplated the tight bandaging that held his left arm firmly against his body. He was grateful that it was his left collarbone rather than his right that bore the break. At least he could still use his right hand.

Nurse Roberts came into the room with a steaming tray of food. "Here we are. This ought to make you feel considerably better. You'll notice that I've brought you some coffee as well. Now can I get you anything else?"

"I appreciate all that you've done. If it wouldn't be too much trouble, I'd be most grateful if you'd get me a Bible," August said, struggling to sit up. "I have some catching up to do."

"Here, let me help you," Nurse Roberts said as she put the tray down. She lifted August with ease and even managed to keep from causing him greater pain.

August looked into the soft brown eyes and sighed. He missed his mother.

"Thank you," August whispered.

"Not at all," the woman said and brought the tray to his bed. "Now you eat everything here, and I'll be happy to search out a Bible for you."

August reached out and placed his hand to cover the older woman's hand. "Would it offend you if I told you that you remind me of my mother?"

The woman broke into a big smile. "Certainly not. Is she nearby? Can I call her for you?"

"She's dead," August said thoughtfully. "No, she's gone, but she's in heaven. She loved God more than anything or anyone, and I know I'll see her again."

"That always makes it easier, doesn't it," the woman observed. "Knowing that your loved ones are safe in the arms of Jesus and that you'll one day see them in heaven—it's all that gets me through each day when I think of those who have gone before me."

"You talk as one who knows," August replied softly.

"I do, son. I do. I lost my husband and children in the influenza epidemic. I decided to train and become a nurse after that. But even after all these years, it hurts to remember them and know that I must wait." The woman's voice was barely audible.

August squeezed her hand. "Someone is always left behind. I guess that's our job."

The woman smiled and patted August's hand. "Of course, you're right. Now you eat, and I'll go find you a Bible."

It wasn't until the next day that August came to realize the doctor had given him a great deal of pain killer. As the medication wore off, deep, penetrating pain filled August's body. He struggled to forget it, forcing his mind away from the hospital and to the small rural village where Beth and the boys lived. He tried to imagine Beth at work and the boys at play.

He was grateful when Nurse Roberts brought him more pain medication. While August waited for the drugs to take effect, he leaned back against the pillows and prayed.

"Dear God, I need to be free from this pain. Such pain and misery takes my mind from the hope that I should have in You." August shifted uncomfortably. "I know I could just as easily be dead or dying— perhaps I really am—but Lord, I want to live. I want to see Beth and the boys, and I want to set things right with them.

"Father, I love Bethany Hogan, and I believe You sent me to her and her children to be a husband and father. I know I've doubted Your blessings, but I don't doubt them any longer. Deliver me, Lord. Deliver me and let me live. Amen."

ten

Beth discarded her mending and sat wringing her hands. She was miserable, her boys were heartbroken, and August was nowhere to be found. She blamed herself for driving him out. The image of August's angry face would forever burn in her memory.

She'd only said the things that needed to be said. She'd never meant to hurt August, but she couldn't be married to a man who was obviously fighting God.

The month had been miserable and rainy, leaving Gerald and Phillip bored and stuck inside. Mrs. Miller had graciously shown up to take the boys to her house, but Beth knew they were pining for August, and it was an impossible void to fill.

Then there was the constant worry of war. The Japanese still held strongholds in the Aleutians, and every day rumors fed fear and anxiety.

The army insisted there wasn't any immediate danger, yet there were practice drills from time to time, reminding everyone that the danger was close enough. Civil Defense officials spoke of blackout drills, insisting everyone have heavy curtains to place at their windows. Bethany wondered at this order, given that they were enjoying close to twenty hours of sunshine a day.

Rationing was tightened, and people were

encouraged to do without and buy war bonds. Beth thought of the soldiers who labored long and hard to build the highway through Alaska. She thought them fortunate that no one was shooting at them while they worked. At least not yet.

People seemed more neighborly than ever, offering food, oil, and whatever help they could spare. In Alaska, life depended upon such generosity, but the war made their dependency upon one another more significant than ever.

The summer had been busier than Beth had expected, and it seemed there was never a moment to call her own. She had taken in laundry for highway workers, prepared baked goods for the army, and always had more requests for rooms at her roadhouse than she had rooms to offer. It kept her mind occupied for the most part, but not her heart.

Every day she passed by August's room, wanting to check whether his things were gone, and every day as she reached for the door handle, she stopped. She'd refused to rent August's room, hoping and praying that he'd return, but deep inside, Beth had lost any confidence in that possibility. Opening the door might prove once and for all that her fears were well founded.

Persistent knocking brought Beth hurrying to the front door, hoping that August had returned. The door opened to reveal Mrs. Miller, and Bethany couldn't hide a frown.

"I'm sorry, dear. Have I caught you at a bad time?" Mrs. Miller asked hesitantly.

Beth immediately felt bad for having given Mrs.

Miller the wrong impression. "No, please forgive me. I'm just a bit preoccupied. Won't you come in?"

"Are you sure I'm not causing you a problem?" the older woman questioned as she followed Beth into the house.

"I'm sure. I must apologize for my demeanor these days," Beth said as she motioned Mrs. Miller to a chair. "Would you like some refreshments? I have lemonade and ginger snaps."

"No, I'm fine. I just wanted to visit with you. I know you haven't been yourself, and I wondered if I might help. I know how tedious widowhood can be."

Beth smiled and swept her blond hair back over her shoulder. "You are such a dear to me, Mrs. Miller. I seriously doubt I would have made it had it not been for you and Granny Gantry and now you."

"You mustn't let the past get you down."

"It isn't that," Beth said and bit her lower lip.

"Then what?" Mrs. Miller asked and reached across to pat Beth's hand. "I know I'm being a nosy old woman, but believe me, there are times when talking to someone who understands helps much more than keeping it bottled inside."

Beth smoothed imaginary lines in her olive green skirt. "It isn't the widowhood that grieves me, Mrs. Miller. The problem does relate to a man, however."

"What widow doesn't have man problems?" Mrs. Miller laughed softly. "What seems to be the trouble?"

"I've fallen in love," Beth said matter-of-factly. "But you mustn't tell anyone."

"Your secret is safe with me," Mrs. Miller insisted. "Now why don't you tell me about it? Perhaps you'll feel better afterwards."

Beth poured out all the details of August's appearance in her life and how her feelings had quickly developed into love. "I care far more than I ever thought possible. When JB died, I feared I could never love another, but God has graciously allowed me to love again."

"Then what's the problem?"

"I'm afraid I sent him packing," Beth said sadly.

"Why? What happened?" Mrs. Miller asked in surprise.

"August has something troubling him. Something that won't allow him to feel the closeness to God that I suspect he once felt. I tried to get him to talk about it, but he grew angry and stormed off."

"That was the day the boys helped me pick berries," Mrs. Miller stated.

"That's right," Beth agreed. "I felt so bad after convincing the boys that August would be here when they returned and then he wasn't. Gerald didn't even talk for two days, and when he finally opened up, all this hurt came pouring out. He felt betrayed, and I had to explain that I was responsible."

"But you weren't," Mrs. Miller said gently. "God is working in August's life. You were simply weeding a garden that God planted long ago. If God is striving to bring August back to the fold, you aren't responsible for anything more than living out God's goodness and standing on His Word. If that drove August away, then it is still part of God's plan."

Beth nodded. "Yes, I'm sure you're right. But—" She paused and lowered her face. "I love him, and

I'm so afraid of losing him. What if he won't ever deal with his problems?"

"If it's meant to be, it will be," Mrs. Miller said firmly. "You must stand strong in your faith. God understands your grief and frustration. Trust Him."

Beth studied the older woman for a moment. Her gray hair had been pinned on top of her head without a single wisp escaping its bounds. It gave Mrs. Miller an extremely well-organized look.

The plump woman was wearing a cream-colored dress with pastel flowers splotching it from neck to knee. She carried an air of respectability and solitude, yet Beth was surprised that Mrs. Miller had never remarried.

"Mrs. Miller, may I ask you something personal?"

The widow nodded. "Certainly. I can probably guess what your question will be. But I have one condition upon which I will insist."

"And what is that?" Beth questioned.

"You must stop with the Mrs. Miller title and call me Hazel."

Beth smiled. "I would love to, Hazel."

"Much better. Now ask your question."

"I just wondered why you've never remarried. After all, you live in an area where women are scarce and the companionship of a wife is highly prized and sought after."

Hazel laughed. "That's true enough, and God knows there have been offers. Mostly men who needed a nursemaid or housekeeper, though. I guess the right man never came along."

"How do you bear the loneliness? I mean," Beth

paused trying to think of a tactful way to speak her mind. "I have the boys as well as the roadhouse, and they keep me busy, but you're down there in town all alone."

The older woman sobered noticeably. "It does get hard, especially at night or in the winter. I've been widowed for over five years, and I don't think I'll ever get used to the winters. They're so cold, dark, and endless. The first year I would cry every time the sun set." Her eyes took on a distant look as she remembered those haunting days.

"You don't have to go on," Beth said sympathetically. "Unless, of course, you want to."

"That's all right," Hazel said and continued. "I know you understand. Those first months, I just wandered around trying to figure out what was what. I kept hearing my Zeke calling me, and when I'd realize it was just my imagination, my heart was heavier than ever. At night, I'd wake and reach out for him, but he was gone. When I'd come fully awake it hurt so much that I wished I'd never wake up again."

"Oh, Hazel," Beth murmured, "I'm so sorry."

"Sometimes I still find myself waiting for him to come home from working his trap lines, but of course he never does," Hazel concluded.

Beth nodded. "I know. I think it would have been harder on me, if JB hadn't already been gone for so long. When he left for duty in the air force, I probably felt his absence worse. When I knew he wasn't coming back, I comforted myself in God and my children, but I still couldn't bear living in the house we'd built together."

"I thought about leaving," the older woman agreed, "but I wanted to stay for the very reasons that you wanted to leave. I needed to feel Zeke close at hand. I needed to know his presence at least until the pain was less. The house was a strong reminder of our love. Every scratch or nick reminded me of something Zeke and I had gone through. I needed the comfort of memories."

"The boys are constant reminders for me," Beth said softly. "And though both bitter and sweet, they have been my lifeline. God was so merciful to give them to me. I don't know how I could have gotten through those first days without their love. They truly sustained me."

"Zeke and I wanted to have children," Hazel said honestly, "but God never blessed us with any. I guess that's why I take such pleasure in your boys. They are such joys to have around and so well behaved. They are a credit to you, Beth."

"Thank you for saying so, but teaching them manners has been the easy part. The hard part is playing both mother and father. I feel that my abilities always fall short of what they need, and now the only man they've truly known as father is gone. How can I possibly help them understand?"

"Trust God and wait, Beth. Trust God and wait," Hazel said firmly.

Beth nodded, but her mind was ever on her sons and their broken hearts.

That night, the silence hung heavy between Beth and her boys. Dinner was eaten with little interest, and when Beth suggested a game of dominoes, the boys only gave it a half-hearted effort. When the clock in the hall chimed nine, Beth ushered her sons to their bedroom.

"Momma, when will August come back?" Gerald questioned as he got ready for bed.

"I don't know, Gerry. He has to work on the road, and that takes him far from us. I don't know if he'll be able to come back any time soon."

"Is he mad at us?" Gerald asked in earnest.

Beth wanted to assure her son that August would never hold malice toward him or Phillip, but the words stuck in her throat. No doubt he was mad at her. He'd been so angry the night he'd left, and Beth was afraid he'd never want to see her again.

"I miss him," Phillip piped up from his bed.

"I know. We all miss August and want him to come back." Beth turned and made a pretense of picking up Gerald's discarded clothes to keep the boys from seeing the tears in her eyes.

"I'm going to ask God to send him back to us," Gerald said as he knelt to say his prayers. "I love him, and I still want him to be my daddy."

"I pray, too," Phillip said, scooting out from under his covers. "I want Daddy."

Beth opened the door and turned off the bedroom light. The boys' kneeling figures were illuminated by the shadowy light from the hallway.

She watched in silence as the boys prayed. Their little-boy voices lifted up pleas of love to their God, a God they trusted without doubt. Could Beth somehow do the same? Was it possible to regain the trust she'd once felt when life was more simple?

Seeing the boys safely tucked in, Beth made her way down the hall and to her desk. She'd long ago given August over to God, and there was nothing to be gained by taking him back.

Resting her head in her arms on the desk, Beth prayed for strength to endure the loneliness and for guidance for August. Wherever he was, God could reach him.

eleven

When Saturday came, Bethany awoke to a strange silence. Straining her ears for the sound of her children, she was more than a little surprised to realize they were quiet.

Enjoying the warmth of her bed, Beth reasoned that the children were simply extra tired. They had, after all, spent most of the previous evening helping Mrs. Miller pick berries again.

She was just fading back into dreams of August when something caught her ear. Bolting upright in bed, Beth waited and listened. Moaning sounds came from the boys' bedroom, and Beth knew instinctively that it was Gerald.

As Beth hastily threw on a robe and tore down the hall, a feeling of dread settled over her. By the time she reached the boys' room, her hands were trembling.

"Why am I so afraid?" she whispered to the air. "Surely he's only had a bad dream." She fought desperately to reassure herself. There was no reason for her uneasiness, yet a mother's heart told her something wasn't right.

She opened the door and found a bleary-eyed Phillip sitting beside his brother's sleeping form. All looked well, at least on the surface.

"Good morning, sweetie. How's Momma's boy?" Beth asked, fluffing her younger son's hair. Phillip scurried off the bed and into his mother's arms.

"Gerry's hot," Phillip said, planting a kiss on his mother's cheek.

"I'm sure he's fine. Let's go see," Beth whispered and shifted Phillip from one hip to the other. His legs draped down the side of her body, reminding Beth that he was quickly passing out of babyhood.

"Gerry," Beth said as she put Phillip on the floor beside the bed and took a seat by her sleeping son. She reached out and brushed back the sandy brown hair that had fallen across Gerald's forehead.

His skin was hot and dry, a sure sign of fever. "Gerry, wake up, honey." Beth shook her son gently.

"Mommy," Gerald moaned and opened fever-glazed eyes. "I hurt, Mommy. My head hurts real bad."

"You have a fever," Beth soothed, checking her son for any other symptoms. There weren't any spots to indicate measles or smallpox, and his body seemed free from any swelling or rashes.

"I'll get you an aspirin and a cool towel. You just rest, Gerry. Phillip and I will take care of you." Beth's calm voice masked the dread in her heart.

Beth carried Phillip from the room, speaking as she made her way to the kitchen. "We'll get Gerry some medicine and then he'll feel better." Phillip nodded as Beth hurried to get the aspirin.

Beth put Phillip down and rummaged through the cupboards until she found a small bottle of aspirins. Putting the medicine in her pocket, Beth then poured a glass of water.

"Me thirsty," Phillip declared as Beth picked up the glass.

"I'm sorry, sweetie. Here, have a drink and then we'll take a drink for brother." Beth waited impatiently as Phillip satisfied his thirst. Then after refilling the glass, she returned to Gerald's bed and gently lifted his head to swallow the tablet.

"Ouchy, ouchy, Mommy. It hurts," Gerald cried, recoiling from her touch.

Phillip had padded down the hall to find his mother bent over Gerald. "He sick, Momma?"

"Yes," Beth whispered. "Your brother is very sick."

"The light hurts my head, Mommy. Please turn off the light," Gerald cried softly.

Beth shook her head. Fever usually caused some pain, but never this much. Something was very wrong. She pulled the heavy curtains across the windows and turned back to face the situation.

"Phillip, I need you to stay here with Gerry while I go get the doctor. Can you do that for me?" she asked the tiny boy.

"I take care of Gerry," Phillip said as he planted himself firmly beside his brother.

"Good boy," Beth said. "Now, it's really important that you stay right here and that you don't get off the bed. Do you understand?"

"I be good, Mommy," Phillip said gravely. "I pray for brother."

"That would be good," Beth agreed. "I'm going to go change my clothes, and I'll check in before I go. I'll be right back."

Beth hurried around her bedroom, mindlessly choosing her gardening slacks and one of JB's old shirts. She quickly tied her blond hair back into a ponytail and made her way down the hall to the boys' room.

A light touch to Gerald's forehead confirmed her fears. The fever was rising. "Phillip, I have to go now. When I come back, I'll fix you a special, big-boy breakfast. Would you like that?"

"Can I have applesauce?" Phillip asked, requesting his favorite food.

"You be a good boy, and you can have whatever you like," Beth replied. "I'll be back in a jiffy."

She hurried down the hall, dreading the desertion of her children. She pulled on socks and boots to wade through the muddy roads of the rain-drenched community, and after one final peek at the boys, she rushed from the roadhouse and ran all the way into town.

Beth marveled at the transformation of her small town. The landscape literally became a sea of tents as the army continued to bring in men and supplies. She picked her way through the mud while soldiers whistled or waved in appreciation of a feminine form. The attention made Beth nervous, but she ignored it. Gerald's restless form filled her mind.

She breathed a sigh of relief upon finally reaching the doctor's office. Pushing open the door and mindless of the mud she tracked into the office, Beth made her way to where a nurse sat writing in a ledger.

"I need to see the doctor," Beth said breathlessly.

"What seems to be your ailment, Miss. . ." the nurse fell silent waiting for Beth to fill in her name.

"Mrs. Beth Hogan," she offered impatiently, "and it's not for me, it's my son. He has a high fever."

"The doctor isn't here right now, but I can send him over as soon as he returns," the nurse replied.

Beth's brow furrowed as she bit her lower lip. "I

suppose I'll have to wait then. Do you have any idea how long it might be?"

"Don't worry," the nurse answered sympathetically, "the doctor is setting an arm on the other side of town. He won't be much longer, and I'll send him right on to you. Now, why don't you tell me everything about your son's illness, and I'll pass the information to the doctor."

"He just woke up with a fever. I didn't bother to take his temperature, but I'm certain it's already very high, and it's climbing."

"Anything else?" the nurse questioned as she jotted the information down.

"He says his head hurts and his eyes are very sensitive to light," Beth replied and added in a near sob, "He's only five."

"Try not to worry, Mrs. Hogan. Tell me where I can send the doctor when he returns."

"I run the Gantry Roadhouse east of town. Just follow the road, and our place is a quarter mile past the crossroads," Beth directed in a trembling voice.

"All right, Mrs. Hogan. You go on back home and I'll do what I can. And Mrs. Hogan," the nurse paused, "please try not to worry. Give your son some aspirin and wash him with a cool cloth."

Beth nodded and made her way back toward home. She'd never run as much as she had this day, and by the time she reached the roadhouse, she was winded and every muscle in her legs ached.

Kicking off her muddy boots and slamming the door behind her, Beth raced to Gerald's bedside. Phillip sat faithfully beside his older brother, wiping the cloth over his forehead.

"What a good boy you are, Phillip," Beth said as she reached down and felt Gerald's brow. He felt as hot as ever, and Beth noticed that he didn't even stir at her touch.

"Come along, Phillip. I'll get you dressed and fix you applesauce pancakes."

"Yummy," Phillip said as he jumped down from the bed. "I took care of brother," he stated simply.

"Yes, you certainly did," Beth replied and helped Phillip off with his nightshirt. She replaced the gown with a shirt and pants and led him to the kitchen.

Beth hastily prepared breakfast between trips to the boys' bedroom. She alternated swabbing Gerald's fiery body and flipping pancakes. She had just placed a plate of pancakes and applesauce in front of Phillip when a knock sounded at the door.

"You stay here and eat. I'm certain that will be the doctor, and I'll have to talk to him about Gerry," Beth said as she left the room.

The doctor stood at the door, and Beth breathed a sigh of relief as she took his coat and showed him to Gerald's room.

"My name is Dr. Stevens," the man said as he began to examine Gerald. "My nurse tells me the boy's symptoms just started."

"Yes," Beth affirmed. "He was fine yesterday, although I do recall he seemed a little tired."

The doctor forced Gerald to sit, causing the boy to cry out in pain. Beth knelt by his side.

"It's all right, Gerry. Momma's here."

"It hurts real bad, Mommy," Gerald managed between his cries.

"Son, can you bend your neck as if you were

going to look down your nightshirt?" the doctor questioned.

Gerald made a valiant effort, but it only caused more pain. "No, no. It hurts," he whimpered. Tears formed in Beth's eyes as she watched her child suffer.

"It's all right, son. I'm a doctor, and I'm going to help you."

Gerald said nothing as the doctor eased him back on the bed. The boy reached out for his mother, and Beth immediately took hold of his hand. She waited in silence while the doctor finished his examination and took Gerald's temperature.

"You just rest now, son. I'm going into the hall with your mother so we can figure out how to make you feel better." The doctor finished putting his instruments into his black bag and motioned Beth to follow him.

Beth knew by the look on the doctor's face that the news would not be good. She felt her knees weaken as she pulled the bedroom door closed behind them.

"I'm afraid your son has all the signs of spinal meningitis," Dr. Stevens began. "I can't be certain without running a number of tests, including a complicated procedure called a spinal tap. I don't have the facilities in town to help your boy."

"What is spinal meningitis?" Beth asked anxiously.

"It's an infection that attacks the membrane surrounding the brain and spine. I'm afraid it's often fatal."

"What am I to do?" Beth questioned frantically. "He has to have help. I don't care what it costs or where we have to go."

"I know. I know," the doctor said as he put his arm around Beth. "What we have to do is get your son to a good hospital."

"But how and where?" Beth asked.

"My suggestion would be Fairbanks. I happen to know there's a supply plane headed there in two hours. I believe we should have your son on that plane."

"Then he'll be there," Beth said, regaining a bit of her composure. "I'll get him ready. Just tell me what to do."

"We'll need to keep him from getting chilled, so bring his blankets. I'll get my nurse to accompany you on the trip. She'll know what to do."

"What about Phillip?" Beth questioned. "He's my younger, and he shares a room with his brother." Fear reverberated in every word.

"He should be fine," the doctor replied, placing a hand on Beth's arm. "We don't quarantine for meningitis because there is no conclusive information about the risk of contagion."

Beth felt only minor relief at the doctor's words. "I'll need to get word to Mrs. Hazel Miller on Second Street. She'll need to come and stay with Phillip. I'm afraid I don't have a telephone. Could you send word to her when you get back into town?" Beth asked hopefully.

"I'd be happy to. I'll also get a couple of soldiers to drive you and your son to the airport. Just wait here until they arrive," the doctor instructed.

"I'll be ready."

An hour later, Beth waved a hesitant goodbye to

Phillip and Mrs. Miller. The soldiers showed up as promised, and with them came the nurse who'd assisted Beth at the doctor's office. The woman literally took over and left Beth with nothing to do but look on in helpless frustration.

The drive to the airstrip was a short one, but to Beth, every minute smothered her in apprehension. The soldiers pulled up next to the transport plane and within moments had moved Gerald and the nurse to the stripped-out fuselage of a Lockheed Vega.

Beth's worried look caught the attention of the pilot. "Don't worry, ma'am. We'll have your boy to Fairbanks in less than two hours."

Beth offered the man a fleeting smile. "Thank you. I know you'll do your best." She allowed him to help her up into the plane, her mind filled with only one thought.

"Dear God," Beth breathed against the drone of the airplane's radial engine, "please help my son. Please heal my baby."

twelve

August rotated his shoulder gingerly and waited for any indication of pain. When none came, he smiled. Finally, he was able to move with nearly the same mobility he'd had before the accident.

He offered a wave to the pilot who'd just landed him at the Northway airstrip, then went in search of the Public Road's office and his boss.

Several minutes later, August was sitting beside the cluttered desk that Ralph Greening continued to work from whenever in Northway.

"Catching up on paper work is worse than dealing with the dirt, rain, and mosquitoes," Ralph griped. "I just got back from our old camp. You certainly gave us a scare," he added, offering August a cup of coffee. "This stuff's getting mighty hard to come by up here, so don't ever say no when somebody offers you a free cup," he teased.

August took the coffee and lifted the mug slightly. "To your health!"

Ralph laughed and joined him in the salute. "And to yours!"

The coffee tasted stale and was only lukewarm, but August didn't care. He was finally going to see Beth again, and he was anxious to complete his work with Ralph.

"Doc says I can go back to work, but nothing too strenuous," August said with a grin. "Whatever that means."

"It might mean that you're not to be dumping Caterpillars over the edge of muddy embankments again." At this both men laughed.

"Yeah, I suppose that's what he meant," August agreed and continued. "Anyhow, the way I see it, it's all up to you. You just tell me where to report, and I'll take care of getting there."

Ralph nodded, but then the thought of Bethany Hogan's hasty retreat from Northway came to mind. He'd only learned of her troubles that morning. His frown and knitted brows caused August to put his coffee mug down.

"What is it? What's wrong?" August asked.

"I went to see Mrs. Hogan today. You know, I wanted to tell her about your accident. I already felt bad that so much time had passed since you were flown to Anchorage, but I had no way of getting back here to tell her," Ralph said apologetically.

"I understand, Ralph, and I'm sure that Beth did," August offered.

"No, she wasn't there," Ralph said with a shake of his head. "Mrs. Hogan had one of her boys take sick. He was pretty bad, and they had to get him to a hospital. They flew out a couple days ago. I think they took him to Fairbanks."

August turned ashen. "Which boy?"

Ralph leaned back and closed his eyes. "I think it was the older one, but I can't be sure. Can't picture him in my mind. You'd best go on down to the roadhouse and ask Mrs. Miller. She's been taking care of the place and the other boy."

August was already on his feet. "I'll do that. I guess

it might be a spell longer before I'll be ready to work after all," August said as he made his way out.

"I kind of figured that," Ralph called after him.

August took off at a full run for the roadhouse. He came up the path panting and out of breath, with an aching in his shoulder that hadn't been there that morning. He pounded on the front door and waited impatiently for someone to open up.

"Why, Mr. Eriksson," Mrs. Miller stated in disbelief. "We thought you'd left for good."

"I was injured in an accident and flown to Anchorage. I just returned not more than a half hour ago, and Mr. Greening tells me that Gerald is sick."

Mrs. Miller nodded, and her eyes turned misty. "Poor little boy," she said in a hushed tone. "The doctor doesn't expect him to make it."

"What?" August nearly yelled the word. "What in the world are you talking about? What's wrong with him?"

"Spinal meningitis," Mrs. Miller said ominously. "Beth flew with him to the hospital in Fairbanks, but the doctor said he might already be too far gone. With meningitis, there's just no way of knowing."

"What about Phillip?" August asked with dread.

"Oh, he's fine," Mrs. Miller answered with a smile. "We've been baking since before light. He's asleep right now, but I could wake him if you like."

August barely heard the words. He felt sick at the thought of Gerald dying and knew that it would be hard to see Phillip just then. He thought of Beth in Fairbanks, bearing alone the burden of her desperately ill child. "No, don't wake him. I've got to get to Beth," he muttered.

"I know it'd mean the world to her," Mrs. Miller said with a bit more composure. "She talked so often about you, wondering where you'd gone and if she'd ever see you again."

August nodded. "I've thought a great deal about her, too. Being in a sickbed does that for you—gives you plenty of time to think about the things you wished you'd done differently."

"I know she'll be needing you now," Hazel replied, touching August at the elbow. "She cares a great deal about you."

"I know," August said, turning to leave.

Hazel called out after him, "Please let us know how Gerald is."

"I'll do that. I only hope I'm not too late," August called over his shoulder as he bid the older woman a hasty goodbye. "Tell Phillip that Daddy was here and that I'll see him real soon."

"I will, Mr. Eriksson. I will," Mrs. Miller called out and waved. She whispered a silent prayer for the man as he rounded the bend and disappeared from view.

God was with August as he hurried back to the airstrip. He managed to secure passage on a plane going to Fairbanks, and after their scenic flight and bumpy landing, August went in search of the hospital.

The Fairbanks hospital wasn't a stately affair, but it was efficient. August hastened to find a nurse who could direct him and then made his way to the room where she said he'd find Gerald and Bethany.

At least he's still alive, August thought as he made his way down the corridor. Through the doorway of

Gerald's room, August saw Beth.

She looked frighteningly small and helpless as she prayed at the bedside of her dying child. He could nearly hear her pleading words as she begged for the life of her son.

Hesitating on the threshold, August wondered how she'd react to his arrival. He glanced at Gerald's pale, nearly lifeless form and back again to the boy's mother. "Dear God," August breathed, "please hear her prayers."

August stepped forward. The noise caught Beth's attention. Her mouth dropped open at the sight of August.

"August," she breathed the word.

Beth looked gaunt and drawn, but August thought her beautiful. He opened his arms, praying that she'd come to him.

Without hesitation, Beth got to her feet, crossed the room, and wearily fell into August's arms. "Oh, August, I prayed you'd come. I prayed that God would find you and deliver you to me. Does that sound hopelessly selfish?" she questioned in a sob.

"He heard your prayers about that and then some," August stated. "I've come back to you, but only because I came back to God first."

Beth pulled back with tears streaming down her face. "Really? Oh, August, that's the best possible news. Now if only. . ."

August cupped Beth's quivering chin in his hand. "If only Gerald would get well," he answered for her.

"Yes," Beth replied. "August, he's so sick, and Dr. Matthews doesn't know whether he can get well or not."

"Is it meningitis as they feared?" August asked softly. He glanced over Beth's shoulders at Gerald.

"Yes," Beth answered and reached up to take hold of the hand that held her. "They sent for an experimental drug from the States, but it hasn't seemed to help."

"Well, we will have to pray together for him," August said tenderly.

Beth closed her eyes and nodded. "I've prayed alone enough for both of us, but I know there's strength in numbers. I'm afraid this time we need all the help we can get."

"Don't worry, Beth. You never have to be alone again. I've done a great deal of thinking and growing up as well. While I had nothing to do but lay in that hospital bed—"

"What?" Beth said pulling away from August. "You were in the hospital? But why? Are you all right?"

"Relax," August said pulling Beth back against him. "I was in an accident a while back. It happened while I was grading the highway. The tractor fell over an embankment that had been weakened by rain. I'm fine now—just a little stiffness in my shoulder and a scar on my head."

Beth's eyes searched for the red welt. She reached up a hand and pushed back August's hair to reveal the scar. "Oh, August!" she exclaimed. "Does it hurt you still?"

"Not much. My collar bone was broken, and it still smarts a bit if I overdo, but really I'm fine. I just didn't want to send a letter to explain all that had happened. I wanted to wait until I could see you in person."

"I thought you hated me and had left for good," Beth blurted out honestly. "I felt so bad for sending you away." She glanced back at Gerald. "The boys were just heartbroken."

August nodded. "I knew they would be, and I hated myself for walking away. I knew I needed to listen, but I couldn't make myself turn around. What you said was exactly what I needed to hear. Of course, I couldn't see that until I was half dead. Then, it was as if God had seen that simple methods wouldn't work with me, and He reached down with something I couldn't ignore."

"He usually does," Beth said with the slightest beginnings of a smile.

August acknowledged her with a smile of his own. "God knew he was dealing a particularly stubborn case. I'd run as far as I could, and when God couldn't pin me down any other way, I guess he used a tractor." August's words were lighthearted in spite of his ordeal.

"I confessed my sins, knowing that the only thing real in my life was my relationship with God. I remembered when my mother had put me on her knee and explained that each of us needed a Savior. 'Some people seek one in a lifestyle or a job,' she said. 'Others try to force people into that role, but what we need is Jesus.'

"I remember even now how amazed I was that Jesus had come to earth to save my soul. It only took remembering that simple wonderment to make me take a more realistic look at what I'd done to myself. You were a brave woman to stand your ground with me, Beth."

Moaning from the bed brought Beth and August to Gerald's side. "I'm not so brave," Beth murmured, looking fearfully into August's eyes. August placed his hand against the boy's fiery brow, while Beth took his hand.

"I'm here, Gerry. Momma's here," Beth whispered softly. Gerald calmed, opened his eyes, then closed them again. Beth began to cry softly. Exhausted by her vigil at Gerald's sickbed, she collapsed across the edge of the bed.

August came and lifted her to her feet. "Beth, come on. You have to rest."

"No! I must stay with him," she protested as August led her from the room. "He might wake up, and I don't want him to be afraid."

"We'll just be down the hall. I'll tell the nurse to watch over him. She'll let us know if he wakes up," August said firmly as he pulled Beth along.

Beth's protests only further weakened her. Finally, she gave up and allowed August to take her to the waiting room. August's strong arms offered her the strength that she'd prayed for. She breathed a prayer of thanks while August helped her to a chair.

"You wait right here, and I'll see if I can't get us a cup of coffee or something," August said.

Beth nodded and watched as he walked to the nurses' station. How grateful she was for his direction and strength. She had been so afraid of never seeing him again, and now, just when God knew she needed August the most, he was at her side.

The aching in her heart refused to abate, however. The doctor had told her there was no hope for her son. No hope whatsoever.

Beth knew better than to give up hope. While there was life, God could work. But it was hard to maintain hope in the face of such devastation. How could she explain to a doctor she'd only met that this child had to live, that without him a part of her heart would be forever broken? He was a man of medicine, and his cold, scientific attitude left Bethany empty.

Her eyes misted at the thought of Gerald's suffering. He was so little and defenseless. He didn't deserve this sickness. Beth felt weak to the point of being sick. How much more could either of them take?

God had heard her prayers, Beth reminded herself. After all, August was here, and he'd renewed his faith in God. God had surely sent August to help her through Gerald's illness. Leaning back against the chair, Beth closed her eyes and tried to pray. She was so tired, so weary of fighting alone.

Within moments, sleep washed over her. August returned to find Beth eased back against the chair sound asleep, but she still wore the worried concern he'd noted when he first saw her at Gerald's bed.

"Give her peace, Father," August prayed as he sat down beside her. "She's remained faithful and true, Lord. Please renew her strength."

thirteen

Throughout the long evening, August maintained his watchful guard over Bethany's sleeping form. He managed to find a blanket to cover her with and continued praying for both Beth and Gerry as she slept.

August watched the seemingly motionless hands on the clock. Nine, then ten o'clock dragged by, and still what sky he could see through the window showed streaks of light. The long summer night made it impossible to judge time.

Eleven, twelve, and finally one o'clock passed without word of Gerald's condition. August hesitated to ask for fear of waking Beth. She needed sleep more than anything else. He'd nearly decided to risk the disturbance when the nurse appeared with Gerald's doctor.

"I'm afraid I have bad news," Dr. Matthews said as he stood before August.

Beth stirred at the sound of voices and sat up. "What is it?" she questioned.

"Your son is failing rapidly. I suggest you and your husband come say your goodbyes," the doctor replied. Neither Beth nor August sought to correct the mistaken reference to their relationship.

Beth began to cry, and August could only hold her close and stroke her head. He turned weary eyes to the doctor before asking, "Are you certain there is nothing else we can do?"

"I'm sorry," Dr. Matthews answered. "It is never easy to tell parents that their child won't make it. Gerald has fought hard to get this far, but he's too weak and the disease is taking too great a toll. He won't make it through the night."

"No, no," Beth sobbed. "He must live. He mustn't die!"

"Mrs. Hogan, please don't do this to yourself. It is of no help to your son. He's beyond our care now, and nothing can be gained by making yourself sick over his passing." The doctor's words seemed callous to Beth.

"You talk as though he were already dead," Beth replied as she pushed August away and got to her feet.

"For all intents and purposes, Mrs. Hogan," Dr. Matthews said without emotion, "he is. I can't do anything more for him. He's not responding to medicine, and his body is too spent to continue fighting. Let him go. You're a young, healthy woman, Mrs. Hogan. I'm certain you and your husband will have other children."

"I want other children, Doctor," Beth said with an undercurrent of anger to her voice. "But not to replace a dead child. I refuse to give up hope that God can deliver my baby from this illness. I have faith that He can work beyond your abilities."

The doctor shrugged his shoulders. "I cannot deny your tenacity, Mrs. Hogan. I only hope that your faith is not misplaced."

"It isn't," Beth stated firmly as she pushed past the doctor and his nurse. "If you can't give me any reason to hope, I know Who can."

August watched as Beth moved down the hall with renewed determination. He turned to the doctor and spoke. "I can understand a portion of your unemotional response to her, Dr. Matthews. You must see dying every day and find it as grotesque and unbearable as I do. However, I will take it as a personal insult should you feel the need to ever resort to crushing her hopes again."

"I assure you, sir," the doctor interjected, "that stripping that young mother of hope was never my intention. She has labored long and hard at the bedside of your child. She has demonstrated a strength beyond human capabilities. I admire all that she has done, but I also want her to understand that there comes a time when nothing more can be done. We have reached that point with your son."

August felt a tug at his heart with every reference to Gerald as his own child. "I cannot accept that the situation is without hope," he stated firmly. "I refuse to believe it."

"Most people do," the doctor agreed. "But people get sick, and people die. We doctors can only do so much. I have done everything in my power, and now I must stand aside and say it is out of my hands."

"You're absolutely right, Doctor. It is out of your hands, but not out of God's." August moved with determined strides to Gerald's room.

When he entered, Beth was stretched out over Gerald's tiny frame. He could hear her praying in a hushed whisper. She was a determined woman, August admitted. She had been determined for him to come back to God, just as she was intent on seeing her son healed of meningitis.

August thought back to those long moments spent beneath the tractor. His accident had opened his eyes to God's love and forgiveness, but it had also given him a glimpse into the power of prayer. Beth had been praying for him. His sister, Julie, and her husband, Sam, had both written letters of encouragement and mentioned their prayers for his well-being. Other people had prayed for August without him being aware of their concern.

That was it! August turned quickly from the room and went in search of a telephone. He would call Julie and ask her to pray for Gerald. He would ask her to gather as many people as possible and get all of them to pray. Then he would call and leave word for Mrs. Miller and the flock that attended church in Northway. There was power in prayer, of this he was certain, and August would leave nothing to chance where Gerald was concerned.

Locating a telephone, August quickly gave the operator all the needed information and waited impatiently while she connected him to his sister.

"Hello," a sleepy Julie sounded on the other end of the phone.

"Julie, it's August. I need you to pray about something!" August knew Julie would have received his letter explaining his return to God and the love he held for Beth and her sons.

"August!" Julie exclaimed. "What's wrong that would have you calling me at this hour?"

"It's Gerald. He's one of the little boys I wrote you about. He's the older boy, and he's terribly ill," August explained.

"What's wrong with him?" Julie asked in an

authoritative voice. Her years as a nurse would require August to give her all the details.

"Spinal meningitis," August spoke the dreaded words.

"How long has he been sick? What have they done for him?"

"I guess he's been sick about three, maybe four days. I just got here myself and don't know what all they've done for him. I heard something about an experimental drug from the States, but the doctor says Gerald isn't responding and that there's no hope. He told us to say our goodbyes."

"How awful," Julie whispered. "I'll be praying for you."

"That's why I called. I want you to pray for a miracle. Beth can't bear losing him, and neither can I. In my heart, he's already my son, and I want God to heal him so I can be a real father to him."

"A miracle is exactly what it will take," Julie said hesitantly. "I know God can do anything, but—"

"No buts," August interrupted. "God can do anything. The doctor may have given up on Gerald, but Beth and I haven't. I want as many people praying and pleading for his life as I can get."

"Then you'll have Sam and me," Julie assured. "I'll even wake up our friends and get them to pray."

"Thanks, Jewels," he replied, using his sister's nickname. "I knew I could count on you. Now, if you don't mind, I'm going to make another call and get back to Beth and Gerald."

"I don't mind at all," Julie replied. "And August," she added, "welcome back to the family. I missed you and your encouraging faith. I knew God would work in a mighty way in your life, just as I know He will work in Gerald's. Goodnight, brother."

"Goodnight, Jewels."

The warmth of his sister's love bolstered his courage, and August quickly made the call to Northway. Ralph Greening readily agreed to trek out into the night and rally the town to pray for Gerald.

Making his way back to Gerald's room, August found Beth sitting beside her son, holding his hand. Her eyes were closed, and August wondered if she'd fallen asleep or if she still prayed. He touched her lightly on the shoulder, and Beth opened her eyes.

"I was worried," she said. "Where were you?"

"I was rounding up support for our efforts," August said with a sheepish grin. "I've rallied the troops, so to speak."

"You've what?" Beth questioned, wondering at August's smile.

"I called my sister in Nome and Ralph Greening in Northway. They're in turn going to rally their friends and ask for prayer for Gerald. We'll have so many requests for healing going before God's throne, we won't be able to count them," August said with contagious excitement in his voice.

"How wonderful," Beth said and dropped Gerald's hand to take August's. "You truly amaze me, Mr. Eriksson. Not long ago you would have scoffed at God's power. Now you call upon it, knowing that even though the doctors have thrown up their hands, God can turn things around."

"I have you to thank for this," August said, pulling Beth into his arms. "You never lost faith that God could turn me around. I simply took that principle and put it into practice."

Beth allowed August to engulf her with his sturdy arms. Her blond hair fell across his arm, glittering like gold in the pale hospital light. She looked up into dark eyes that bathed her in love. Silently, she thanked God for answering her prayers for August's change of heart and then thanked God for hearing her prayers for Gerald. She felt hesitant at the latter, but it seemed important to trust God for those answers.

August felt his heart nearly burst with love for the woman he held. He longed to convey those feelings and ask Beth to marry him, but he knew the moment wasn't right. He didn't want her to say yes out of gratitude for his presence. Nor did he want her to refuse him because of the strain of Gerald's ordeal.

"I hate waiting," August murmured. Beth assumed his words were about Gerald's condition.

"I know. God has things under His watchful eye, but it doesn't always seem that way as we wait and wonder," Beth replied.

"Waiting all these years for someone or some purpose to come into my life has been difficult, too," August said cautiously.

"But now that you've waited, God has been faithful to send you people who care for you and love you," Beth whispered as she hugged herself close to August. "That little boy loves you nearly as much as I do. You mean the world to him, and I can't imagine God allowing Gerald to die without knowing that you're back here with him."

"All of this is a testing time," August stated firmly. "A time of trial such as Jesus said we'd experience in this world. But Jesus also said we could be of good cheer for He'd already overcome this world."

Beth nodded. "I believe that," she said, pulling away. "I believe that we will overcome this situation and that God will bless our boy." Beth thought fleetingly of JB and knew in her heart that he would approve of August as father to his son.

"Come on," August said and pulled Beth with him to Gerald's bedside. "Let's join our friends and pray for Gerald."

fourteen

It was close to three o'clock in the morning when Dr. Matthews reappeared to check Gerald's condition. The nurse ushered Beth and August into the hall while he conducted his examination. Within moments, the nurse brought them back. The doctor was writing notes on Gerald's chart.

Beth immediately went to Gerald's side, while August followed the doctor into the hall.

Dr. Matthews opened his mouth to speak, but August held up his hand. "There's nothing you can say. I know the odds are against that child. I know all of your medical expertise and skills have been tested and tried. Furthermore, I realize that even faithful servants of God lose loved ones in death. It's part of life."

August paused, pushing his hands deep into his jean pockets. His face took on a thoughtful look. "However, I also know the power of prayer."

Then with a smile of sudden peace on his face, August added, "Gerald's going to make it, and of that, I'm certain. He's going to get well because God will heal him."

Without waiting for a reply from the doctor, August turned back into the room, passing the nurse as she was leaving. August wanted to share his new feelings of peace with Beth. He entered the room and paused as Beth lovingly wiped her son's forehead.

"Gerry," August could hear her saying. "It's Momma, Gerry. I need you to get well. I'm asking God to make you well because He said I could ask for anything in Jesus' name and He would hear me. I'm doing that Gerry. I'm asking in Jesus' name that, your life be spared."

August could bear no more. "Beth, I know God will make Gerald well. I feel a calm and peace about it."

Beth stopped praying and looked up at August. "Honestly? You aren't just telling me that to give me hope?"

"I am telling you that to give you hope, but only because it's true. I feel such confidence that I want to sing it out. I even told the doctor that God would make Gerald well."

Beth crossed the room to where August stood. "I want to believe that, August. I know God is capable, but is He willing?"

"I believe He is," August replied. He looked into Beth's eyes and prayed she'd see the confidence in his own.

"Then I'm no longer worried," she said slowly. "If God has given you that certainty, then I shall praise Him for it and await my son's healing. I will believe!"

"That a girl!" August said pulling Beth into his arms. "You're something special, Bethany Hogan."

Together they prayed and kept vigil at Gerald's bedside. Pulling chairs alongside the bed, August and Beth sat together, holding each other's hands and Gerald's as well.

Shortly before dawn, August and Beth awoke. Gerry

seemed to be in a deep, natural sleep. Beth reached out and touched the brow of her son.

"Oh, August!" she exclaimed. "He's not at all feverish. And look," she pointed to his chest. "He's not straining to breathe."

August stared at the rhythmic rise and fall of the tiny chest and nodded. "He's getting well, Beth. God is healing him even as we watch."

"Thank You, God," Beth said as tears ran down her cheeks. "Thank You for the life of my baby."

"Amen," August said in agreement.

Taking Beth with him to the window, August pulled back the heavy drapes to reveal a glorious sunrise bursting from the horizon. He reached out and wiped away Beth's tears. "Joy has truly come in the morning, just as the psalmist said. No more tears, Bethany. Now we will rejoice."

Beth nodded and threw her arms around August's neck. "I will spend the rest of my life rejoicing for the miracles of God," she whispered.

Just then another voice joined in. "Mommy!" Gerald called out. His voice sounded hoarse but strong.

Beth and August rushed to Gerry's side and found him not only awake, but also free of the glassy-eyed, feverish look. Staring in amazement, August and Beth could only smile.

"How do you feel, son?" August asked as he bent over the boy.

"Daddy," Gerald said forgetting himself. "You came back. I thought maybe you didn't like me any more."

"That could never happen, Gerald," August replied.

"I was very far away in a hospital, much like this one."

"A hospital?" Gerald questioned. "What's a hospital?"

"Oh, Gerry," Beth said as she sat down beside him. "A hospital is a place for sick people to get well. You've been very sick, but God has made you well."

"I had nice dreams," Gerald said surprising them both. "I dreamed about lots of pretty flowers and a big river. Bigger than the one Phillip fell into."

Beth glanced in amazement at August and then back to her son's shining face. "I'll bet it was wonderful," she replied. "I'm so glad you're feeling better," she added placing a kiss on his forehead.

"Me, too. I'm hungry, Mommy. Can I have some breakfast?" Gerald asked.

August laughed loudly. "Spoken like a true boy."

"Always hungry," Beth admitted. "We'll see if we can't manage to find something for you to fill that empty tummy of yours."

"I'll go right now and speak with the doctor," August said. But before August had made it to the door, Dr. Matthews entered the room and stared in shocked surprise at the sight of Gerald sitting up in bed.

"What's going on?" the doctor asked as he crossed the room.

"I told you God would make him well," August said with a hearty slap on the doctor's back.

"It's impossible," the doctor whispered in amazement. "That child should be dead by now." His words were spoken so softly that only August could hear them.

"Well, he isn't. In fact, he's very much alive and very hungry," August informed the man. Gerald agreed with an enthusiastic nod of his head.

"I simply don't believe it," Dr. Matthews said, walking over to Gerald's bed.

"Many people never do," Beth said firmly, refusing to take her eyes from her son's face. "And because of that, they never know the fullness of God's powerful love."

The doctor shook his head as he examined Gerald. He took a thermometer from his medical bag and put it into Gerald's mouth. While he waited for the results, the doctor felt for a pulse. His eyes registered surprise when he found a strong, steady beat.

Taking the thermometer from Gerald's mouth, Dr. Matthews again shook his head. "It's normal, and his pulse is strong and steady," he said, looking to Beth and August as if for an explanation.

"God has worked a miracle, Doctor," Beth said as she tousled Gerald's hair. "He has given me back my son."

The doctor nodded. "I suppose you're right." He had Gerald bend his head back and forth and from side to side. When he was satisfied that no symptom of the meningitis remained, he declared the boy could eat some breakfast.

Beth and August joined Dr. Matthews at the door of Gerald's room. "I'll need to run some more tests, but I must say, I am completely amazed," the doctor said humbly. "I have never seen God work a miracle such as this in the life of anyone, let alone one of my patients. Makes me feel rather useless."

"We want to thank you for all you did to help

Gerald," Beth said as she extended her hand. "We know you did what you could, and we don't believe it useless for one moment. You simply operated under human limitations. We took it beyond that and expected divine results." Beth's words were gentle and supportive.

August nodded as his arm encircled Beth's waist. "If we could do everything ourselves, there'd be no need for God. Since we can't, we must turn to Him on a daily basis and pray for guidance, strength, and direction. I hope you feel inspired by this miracle."

"I certainly feel a wonderment about it," the doctor admitted. "It's like nothing I've ever seen, and it certainly bears consideration. Now, if you'll excuse me, I'll send a nurse in with a breakfast tray."

Beth smiled. "I know that'll make Gerry a very happy boy." The doctor nodded and turned down the hall, a baffled look covering his face.

"I guess that'll teach him to question a woman of faith," August said with a laugh as they turned back to Gerry.

"Where's my brother?" the boy asked eagerly. He was already trying out the bounce in the hospital mattress.

"He's back at the roadhouse with Mrs. Miller," Beth explained. "This hospital is in Fairbanks."

"That's far, far away from home," Gerald said, amusing both August and Beth. "How did I get here?"

"We took the airplane," Beth answered. "The soldiers helped us get here. Do you remember anything at all?"

"Nope," Gerald replied. "I just remember sleeping and sleeping. I'm glad you came back, August.

You aren't going to leave again, are you?"

"No," August said, reassuring the child. "I don't plan on being far from you ever again."

"Good," Gerald said with a grin. "It made my Mommy sad when you went away."

"Gerald!" Beth said with a finger to her lips. "You mustn't tell August about all that."

"Of course he must," August said with a grin to match Gerald's. He lowered his head to Gerald's and added, "I want to know everything that happened while I was away."

Beth shook her head at the grinning faces. "It isn't the past that matters," she chided with a smile. "It's the future that counts, and I intend that we should have a glorious one."

"I agree," August said, holding his hand out to Beth. "You can tell me all about it later," he added with a wink to Gerald.

"You are quite impossible, Mr. Eriksson," Beth said in mock exasperation.

"Not at all, Mrs. Hogan," August said as he lifted Beth's hand to his lips. "Just determined."

The touch of his lips on Beth's hand caused her to tremble. She could feel her pulse race and her breathing quicken. For the first time, nothing stood between her and August.

As if reading her thoughts, August smiled. He could feel her quiver at his touch. His eyes met hers, and in their reflection he saw all of his long-held dreams coming true.

"When's the food going to get here?" Gerald interrupted. "I want to eat, and then I want to go home."

August and Beth laughed and pulled Gerald into their arms. "I think that sounds wonderful," Beth agreed.

fifteen

Several bowls later, Gerald gobbled down oatmeal with raisins while Bethany told him about his days spent in the hospital. Meanwhile, August made arrangements for their trip home. He felt a lightheartedness he'd never known.

"Julie?" August spoke into the receiver of the phone. "It's August."

"August, how's the little boy?" Julie questioned through a static-filled line.

"He's fine. We got our miracle, Julie. Gerald rallied in a remarkable way," August replied.

"Praise God," Julie replied. "I knew He'd hear our prayers. How is Beth?"

"She's exhausted, but otherwise great. You would like her, Jewels. She has a strong faith just like you. She never doubted that God could make a difference," August said with pride.

"She sounds like the perfect woman for you," Julie remarked. The static played havoc with the line. "I'm sorry about the connection. I don't know if it has anything to do with it or not, but we're in the middle of a fierce storm. High winds and snow. You know the type."

"I do indeed. The temperature's dropped considerably here, but good weather is holding which is another blessing. They're still trying to finish up the highway. I think they'll be done within a matter of a week or so," August replied.

"Will you be coming home after that?" Julie asked hopefully.

"I'd just begun thinking about that," August answered. "I want to come back, at least to get my things. I miss my dogs, and I want to teach the boys how to drive a sled."

"We'll look forward to seeing you," Julie said enthusiastically. "Sam has missed you a great deal," she added, referring to her husband.

August thought of how much Sam would have enjoyed working on the highway. "I've missed him, too. Tell him hello and that I'll see you both soon. I'll talk to you again before I actually come back. Thanks again, Jewels."

"I'm glad we could be a part of your miracle," Julie replied. "It was good to hear your voice. Please take care of yourself."

"I will. I love you, Sis."

"I love you, too. Goodbye." Julie's voice was barely audible through the static.

After another quick call to Ralph Greening, August was free to return to Beth and Gerald.

"It's all set," August said as he entered the room. "As soon as the doctor gives his approval, we'll be on the first transport plane for Northway."

Gerald had finished his breakfast and waited eagerly for his mother's permission to get out of bed.

"Dr. Matthews said we could leave as soon as he has one of the other doctors take a look at Gerald," Beth said with a smile.

August looked at her with appreciation. Now that his own bitterness toward God and Gerald's serious

illness no longer filled his mind, August was beginning to recognize the perfection of the woman
before him. She was everything he'd ever needed or
wanted.

"Did you hear what I said?" Beth questioned.

"Huh? No, sorry. What did you say?" August asked
as he crossed the room.

Beth laughed. "It wasn't important. I have you and
Gerald, and soon we'll go home to Phillip. That's
what matters."

Dr. Matthews came into the room unannounced
just then. With him was an elderly man Beth didn't
recognize.

"This is Dr. Barnes," Gerald's doctor announced.
"I've asked him to evaluate our patient and give his
opinion."

"How nice to meet you, Dr. Barnes," Beth said as
she extended her hand. "So you've come to see our
miracle boy."

"Yes, Mrs. Hogan," the man said, shaking her hand.
"I must say, I was quite enthralled by the boy's
recovery. I understand your son was only two days
on the experimental medicine from the States."

"Yes, that's true," Beth said and added, "but I don't
believe that's what cured him. After all, you folks
had given him up for dead."

Dr. Barnes picked up Gerald's chart and studied it
for a moment. Gerald finally broke the silence. "Are
they going to let me go home, Momma?"

"I think so, Gerry, but you must be quiet and let
the doctors do their job," Beth replied, giving her
son a hug.

Dr. Barnes continued his examination of Gerald

and finally turned back to Beth with a smile. "I see no reason to keep this child here any longer. Your son is completely healed to the best of my knowledge."

"Thank you," Beth replied. She threw a knowing smile at August, who had held back in silence while the men examined Gerald.

August stepped forward and put an arm around Beth. "How soon can we leave?" he asked.

"As soon as you're ready," Dr. Barnes replied. "I release the boy as of now."

Gerry let out an excited scream at the verdict, and August and Beth thanked the doctors once more for their help as the medical men turned to leave.

When the doctors had left, August turned to Beth. "Ready to go home, Mrs. Hogan?"

"Definitely," she replied, taking his offered hand.

August and Beth hugged Gerald close. August silently thanked God for the loving family He'd provided.

"You know," August began, "I think we should have a word of prayer and thank God for all He's done for us. Then I think we should get out of this hospital and head home to Phillip and Mrs. Miller."

"I agree," Beth said, lifting her eyes to August. In that moment she wanted nothing more than to spend the rest of her days loving this man and her children.

"Father, we come to You with thankful hearts," August began. "We praise You for the healing of Gerald's body and for the mercies You showed me in bringing me back to the truth."

Beth listened intently as August prayed, agreeing with his words and enjoying the blessings of God's love. Silently, she added her own requests.

I love him, Lord, she prayed. *I love him so very much, and if it is Your will, I pray You'll see us married quickly so that we can be a whole and complete family.*

August ended his prayer and Gerald joined in with a hearty "Amen." Beth lifted her face to reveal tears that she'd not realized she had cried.

"Why are you crying, Mommy?" Gerald asked with a worried look on his face. "Is something wrong?"

August turned, seeing the tears for the first time. "I think your mommy is happy, Gerald. Sometimes folks have a hard time expressing the wonder of how happy they are."

Beth dabbed her eyes with the corner of a handkerchief that August offered her. "I am happy, Gerry. I'm so very glad that God has made you well and that He brought August back to us."

She turned to August, feeling confident for the first time that she could speak what was on her heart. "Please don't leave us again. We need you. I need you."

Beth's blue eyes pierced deep into August's heart. Years later he would remember the moment as one of the most precious in his life. She was so needy, yet so strong. Somehow, the two qualities balanced perfectly, creating one incredible woman.

"And I need you," August whispered, his dark eyes shining with love. "I'll always need you."

Gerald refused to be left out of the conversation. He was bored with the adult seriousness. "Can we go home?" he asked breaking the spell of the moment.

"I want to play in my treehouse."

Beth laughed, and August lifted Gerald into his strong arms.

"Yes," August said enthusiastically. "Let's go home!"

sixteen

From Fairbanks to Northway, Gerald chattered about the plane and the view. August pointed out the highway below and explained to the boy about the work involved in building such a road.

Gerald listened in awe as August spoke of the powerful machinery that helped clear the way. "I'd like to do that too," Gerald said in animated excitement. "I want to do work just like you."

"I thought you wanted to be a pilot," August replied, shifting Gerald so he could get a better view.

"That was what my old daddy did. Now I want to do work like my new daddy. You are going to be my new daddy, aren't you?" Gerald questioned sincerely.

"Would you like that?" August asked with a grin.

"I sure would," Gerald answered. "Phillip would, too. He told me so."

"Well then," August said with a glance at Beth, "we'll just have to see what the good Lord works out."

Beth felt a twinge of disappointment at August's words. She'd held her breath, waiting for his reply, and then she'd only heard a "wait and see" answer. Hiding her frustration, Beth was relieved that Gerald seemed satisfied with August's answer.

Folding her hands in her lap, Beth thought about the situation and glanced up to find August watching her. She offered the briefest smile, and when

August winked and grinned back, Beth felt relieved. There was no way of knowing exactly what August had in mind, but Beth was certain he loved her and the boys. Wait and see wasn't an easy thing to accept, but it did offer the possibility of more, and Beth clung to that for reassurance.

The plane touched down shortly before dinner time with Gerald already complaining that his stomach was growling. Stepping off the plane, August offered a hand to Beth.

"It's good to be home," Beth declared and breathed deeply of the crisp air. "I've missed it so much and Phillip, too."

August easily lifted Gerald into his arms and swung in step behind Beth. "I suggest we get your things, and I'll see about securing us a ride home. After all, this little boy is about to starve to death."

"I'll square getting the suitcase," Beth offered with a laugh. She watched as August hoisted Gerald over his head and onto his shoulders. What a great father he would be for her sons!

August waited until Beth was deep in conversation with the pilot before going off in search of a ride to the roadhouse. It was hard to believe that autumn had come in their absence. The fireweed was snowy with its cotton plumes floating through the air, and aspen shimmered with their hues of gold and orange.

In the distance, August could see that the Wrangell Mountains were already glistening with thick layers of snow. It wouldn't be long before snow would hug the ground in a white, insulating blanket. Thoughts of cold weather made August think of his dogs and sled travel. He'd have to find a way to bring them here from Nome and teach the boys to drive a team.

It wasn't hard to find a ride to Gantry Roadhouse; most everyone had heard of Gerald's illness and were anxious, even pleased, to lend a hand to the little boy.

The driver of the jeep turned out to be Private Ronnie Jacobs, one of the soldiers Beth had baked sweet potato pies for.

"It's mighty good to see that your boy is healthy and strong again," Ronnie said as he helped Beth into the seat.

"Thank you, Private," Beth returned. "Have they kept you well fed in my absence?"

The young man laughed. "Not on this army's food. I missed coming down to the roadhouse to buy the extras. I guess pretty soon we'll be out of here altogether. It'll sure be good to go back where it's warm. I miss Georgia."

"Who's she?" Gerald asked as August handed him to Beth.

Ronnie laughed. "That's not a girl. It's the state I live in."

"Is it as pretty as Alaska?" Gerald asked.

"I think so," the private responded taking the driver's seat while August jumped in the back. "Now, if everybody's set, I'll get y'all home."

The drive to the roadhouse was over quickly. August had barely put a foot out of the jeep when Phillip came bursting out the doorway.

"Mommy! Daddy!" he called out. Running down the dirt pathway, he held out open arms for August's embrace. August tossed him high in the air. Phillip's giggles sounded like music to Beth and August's ears.

"Phillip, you must have grown six inches since I

last saw you. Come give Mommy some love," Beth said, reaching out to take her son from August.

"I missed you, Mommy. I missed you whole bunches." Phillip's muffled voice fell in kisses against his mother's neck.

"Oh, and I missed you, pumpkin. I missed you so much," Beth replied. "And look here," she said as she put Phillip down. "Gerry's back, and he's all better."

"I helped take care of him, didn't I, Mommy?" Phillip questioned, catching sight of his brother. "Gerry!" he squealed as he rushed to hug his sibling. The boys were great friends and had missed each other terribly. Soon they were laughing and talking at once as they shared their adventures with each other.

Mrs. Miller came outside to join the reunion. "Gerald!" she called out and waved. As the foursome approached the older woman, Beth could see there were tears in Hazel Miller's eyes.

"Praise be to God!" she exclaimed embracing Gerald.

"I was real sick," Gerald explained seriously.

"You sure were," the older woman agreed. "But God made you well, and I've made a celebration dinner to thank Him."

"Hazel, how nice!" Beth remarked. She was weary to the bone and anxious to drop into bed, but she wouldn't have spoiled Hazel's celebration for all the world.

"I could eat a moose," August declared with a grin.

"Well, I just might have some of that, too," Mrs. Miller said, laughing. "You'll just have to wash up and set yourself down to see."

The boys and August hurried in the direction of the washroom while Beth lingered a moment with Hazel.

"Hazel, I'm indebted to you for life," Beth said as she hugged her friend. "Without you I would have worried constantly about Phillip and the property."

"I'm happy to have helped. I finally felt useful, and I think it taught me something else," Hazel said, taking a step back.

"And what's that, Hazel?" Beth questioned.

"I've just been wasting myself and the talents the good Lord gave me. I've been hiding myself away, picking and choosing from what I'll be a part of and what I won't. I hadn't realized how cloistered away I'd become."

"Don't be too hard on yourself, Hazel," Beth interjected. "You have done much to live for God. You teach Sunday school at the church and sing in the choir. Everyone who knows you or has had an opportunity to speak with you knows your heart."

"That may be, but I know I can do more and I intend to," Hazel replied. "But enough about me. What about you and Mr. Eriksson?"

"Oh, Hazel," Beth said, smiling broadly. "God has renewed August's heart. He's found his way back to the truth, and he loves me."

"How wonderful!" Hazel exclaimed. "God truly has answered our prayers. Has the man asked you to marry him?"

"Not in those words, but I am certain it's his intention. I can hardly wait until we're a family," Beth said happily.

"I believe you already are," Hazel stated and pulled open the door. "Now come along. My fine supper is getting cold, and those men of yours looked mighty hungry." Beth nodded with a smile and followed Hazel to the kitchen.

Dinner was as fine an affair as any Beth or August had ever known. Hazel had prepared so many specialties that Beth lost track of what she'd sampled.

Smoked reindeer sausages lay in long, steaming strips atop a bed of seasoned rice, while another pot held sliced moose in a tantalizing barbecue sauce.

Sourdough bread from a starter Mrs. Miller claimed was over seventy years old was quickly devoured with huge spoonfuls of homemade blueberry jelly.

Accompanying all this richness was an array of vegetables and fruit that bowed the table under its weight. On top of the stove sat strawberry-rhubarb pies and a fresh pot of coffee. There was decidedly more food than five people could eat, but no one seemed to mind.

"I know you'll want to put those boys to bed," Hazel said as she began to clear the table. "Why don't you run on ahead and take care of them? I'll clean up this mess."

"I can't let you go on taking care of us," Beth said, stacking the boys' dishes together and reaching for August's.

"Now, I'll be gone in an hour or two and you'll have yourself and your family to take care of. Let me do this for you while you enjoy getting back to your routine," Hazel insisted.

"I think that's mighty fine of you, Mrs. Miller,"

August said. He got to his feet and patted his stuffed stomach. "I can't remember the last time I had anything quite that good. After they get done with rationing, you ought to open up a restaurant."

"I think that would be a grand idea, Hazel. Maybe that's the purpose you've been looking to fill," Beth remarked. "Better yet, maybe we could add it to the roadhouse. I know my boarders would be a lot happier if I offered meals with their rooms."

"And if you were careful with the things you served, you could probably get started before the war is over," August said, contemplating the possibilities. "We could build on to the kitchen, maybe over here." August walked to the south wall of the kitchen where the stove stood. "I don't think it would be all that difficult."

"I don't expect you to alter your roadhouse for me," Hazel replied evenly, but in her heart was born the first ray of excitement.

"It would be beneficial to both of us," Beth replied. "Besides, I don't expect to run a roadhouse all of my life. Maybe you could eventually buy me out."

Beth's revelation was news to August. He wondered what her plans were for the future.

"Well, you've certainly given an old woman a great deal to think about," Hazel murmured, moving the hot food back to the stove. "But right now, you have two boys who are nearly asleep as they stand," she said and motioned to where Gerald and Phillip were swaying on their feet.

"Come on, boys," August said, scooping a child into each arm. "I think it's time to tuck you in."

The boys needed little in the way of tucking in. They were both asleep almost before their heads hit the pillows. Beth stood for a moment at the door of their bedroom. She took a deep breath and sighed. The boys slept healthy and comfortable in their beds, and in the kitchen, August waited for her to join him. What more could she possibly want?

Gently, she pulled the door closed and went to August. "Seeing my children at rest has to be the most precious moment of the day. I never fail to be amazed at the comfort and joy it gives me," Beth said, taking August's hand in her own.

Thinking they would be helping clean up the dishes, Beth registered surprise as August maneuvered her past Hazel with a wink and out the back door into the chilly night air.

They walked hand in hand for several yards, enjoying the solitude of the moment. Beth felt a peace she hadn't dared hope for after JB's death.

Pausing, she turned to face August. "I want to thank you for all you've done—especially coming to me in Fairbanks. I think I would have fallen apart if you hadn't been there."

August's dark eyes stared down at her for a long time before he spoke. He was eager to make Beth his wife, yet there seemed so much that had gone unsaid between them. "I needed to be there," he finally whispered, "as much as you needed me to be there."

Beth silently hoped that August would take this opportunity to propose to her. She felt light and airy, and her heart was fairly flying on wings of its own. Surely August felt the same.

Leading Beth to the long bench he had made for

evenings such as this one, August searched for the right words to speak what was on his heart. "I brought you out here for a purpose," he began. "I needed to tell you something and explain."

Beth's brow furrowed. This didn't sound like the beginning of a marriage proposal. "What is it, August?"

"I'm going back to Nome," he replied.

Beth felt her chest tighten. Her mind whirled in a thousand directions as she wondered what August meant by his words. She gripped the arm of the bench and forced herself to be silent. Had she misunderstood his words in Fairbanks? Didn't he intend to marry her after all?

"I have an entire life back in Nome that you know nothing about," August explained. "I have a sister and a lifetime of mementos, not to mention a dog sled team to rival any in the territory."

August's words held such longing that Beth couldn't maintain her silence. "You're leaving us?" She dreaded hearing the answer.

"Only to get my things," August said with a grin. "You can't get rid of me that easily. I don't intend to be gone a moment longer than is necessary to pack my sled and mush my team back here." August noticed Beth's look of concern. "You didn't really think I'd leave you for good, did you?"

Beth shrugged her shoulders. "I didn't know what to think. I mean, I knew how I felt, and I thought I understood how you felt, but—"

"But then I told you I was going to Nome," August interrupted, "and you started to worry?"

"Nome is hundreds of miles away," Beth said,

feeling little relief that August intended to return. "So much could happen to you on the way back. There's so much open, empty space between here and there. What if you have an accident or a storm comes up?"

"I've traveled those trails hundreds, even thousands of times. I know every inch of land between Nome and Nenana. Nothing is going to happen to me," August insisted.

"I wish you didn't have to go," Beth replied honestly. "I've said too many goodbyes."

"Then we won't say goodbye," August stated firmly. "You could come with me. Mrs. Miller could watch over the roadhouse. We could fly to Nome and mush the dogs back together."

Beth shook her head. "I couldn't leave the boys that long. They need me to be a constant in their lives. They've said goodbyes, too, remember? And their father never came home again. I couldn't put them through that, and taking them on the trail would be much too difficult, especially with Gerald just recovered from meningitis."

"I guess I wasn't thinking," August offered by way of apology.

"It's all right. I understand you have to go back, and you understand I have to stay. I guess the thing for me to do is give you over to God once again," Beth said, fighting tears that threatened to spill from her eyes.

"Who better to place me with?" August said, putting his arm around Beth's shoulders. He lifted her face to meet his and spoke with such tenderness that Beth thought her heart would burst. "I love you, Bethany Hogan. I've loved you for so long now, I don't remember a time when I didn't love you. And I love your children as if they were flesh of my flesh. I want to be a father to those boys, and I want to live my life in the warmth of your love."

Without waiting for her reply, August lowered his lips to kiss her long and deeply. He felt her tears fall against his cheek as she clung to him.

When he lifted his face, August was surprised to find Beth smiling. "Tears and smiles?" he questioned. Gently he brushed away a glistening drop from her face.

"I love you, August," she whispered in a voice more composed than August thought possible, given her reaction to his news. "I know your trip is necessary, but I wish you didn't have to leave me for so long."

"I'll be back before you know it, and when I return, I'll bring my mother's wedding rings and marry you. That is, if you'll have me," he added with a broad smile.

Beth reached out to push back his dark hair. The light from the moon illuminated his face as if it were day. "I'll marry you, August Eriksson. I'll be your wife, and bear your children, and all of my days I will love you as I have loved no other."

seventeen

August spent the final days of the highway project behind a desk. After eight months of tedious work and precarious conditions, the Alaskan/Canadian Highway was completed. Nicknamed the Alcan by those who worked it, the roadway was a miracle of cooperative countries and their people.

Destiny's road stretched over nearly fifteen hundred miles and constituted the efforts of more than eleven thousand individuals.

It wasn't much to look at, August decided as he flew from one isolated airstrip to the next, surveying the wonder from the air. Little more than a dingy brown ribbon, it wove its way through the countryside. Occasionally, strips of grey or blue indicated a lake or river, while either side of the narrow highway was lined with dark spruce forests and snow-filled permafrost meadows.

The army was pleased with the accomplishment. The road provided a way to transport oil and other goods to far north bases, should the shipping lanes become too dangerous. But an unanticipated benefit was what a morale booster the road had become. It proved to two nations and millions of their citizens that they could combine their energies on the home front to aid their loved ones serving in battles so far away. It made the people feel important, useful, and necessary for the war effort.

August smiled as the plane touched down in Northway. This was his final official duty for the project. After great consideration and prayer, August had decided against taking the permanent job offered by Ralph Greening.

Instead, August had shared with Beth his desire to raise sled dogs and help her with the roadhouse. She had enthusiastically agreed to having him around the house on a daily basis and had even begun to make a list of jobs August could be responsible for. August had laughed when he learned of the list.

"Good to know I'll be needed," he'd ruefully observed.

The weather had turned cold. Excitement gripped the town of Northway as it bustled with activities commemorating the new highway. But the dropping temperatures and significant snows signaled to August that it was time to go to Nome and retrieve his property. Once done with this, he would settle down to a new life with Beth and the boys.

August shook his head in amazement, remembering his first day in Northway when he was seeking a job on the highway. The road had given destiny to more than the countries through which it passed. God had used it to bring August his own destiny and a new life.

Snow blanketed the ground around the airstrip, leaving August to tramp out his own way to the cross-roads. He didn't mind; it reminded him of days out on the trail hunting or checking trap lines. Remembering his father and the home he'd known as a boy, August was filled with longing to return to that life.

Nearing the roadhouse, August paused in order to

take the sight in. Nestled among the tall spruce and leafless aspen and birch was the place he now called home. Black smoke rose from the chimney, contrasting against the grey, snow-heavy sky. The sight warmed August and prompted him to hasten his steps to the family he'd soon call his own.

Kicking off his snowy boots, August entered the roadhouse through the back door and pulled off his parka to hang it beside Beth's at the entrance to the kitchen. He was surprised to find Beth and the boys sitting at the table, smiling up at him as if they knew a secret.

"What?" August asked with a grin. "What are you up to?"

Phillip and Gerald giggled, while Beth lowered her eyes to keep from laughing out loud. August joined them cautiously at the table and looked on his chair for any sign of a pine cone or other such souvenir of the boys' mischievous behavior. Finding none, he sat opposite Beth, between the boys.

"Is somebody going to tell me what's going on here?" he asked, reaching for Phillip. "Or am I going to have to tickle it out of you?"

"Don't tell him, Phillip," Gerald squealed.

Phillip laughed in glee as August's fingers found his ribs. "Mommy told us you're going to stay and be our daddy," Phillip laughingly gave up the secret.

"She said you had to go to your old house and get your stuff, but that you were coming back to live here with us," Gerald added.

Beth looked at August with a shrug. "I couldn't help telling them," she replied. "And since you never said I couldn't, I gave in to my joy and let them be part of it."

August laughed as he reached out and pulled Gerald to his lap. Holding each boy on a knee, August gave them a squeeze. "And what do you boys think of that?" he asked.

"We like it!" Gerald exclaimed and Phillip echoed.

"Well, that's certainly a good thing for me," August proclaimed. "I guess I would have had a lot of trouble on my hands if you had said you didn't want me."

"I don't want you to go, Daddy," Phillip said with a pout.

"Me neither," Gerald agreed. Beth's expression confirmed that she felt the same way.

"Look, boys," August began, "I'm not going to be gone very long, and when I get back I'm going to be bringing my dog team. I'm going to teach you the old-fashioned way of getting around in the snow."

"We've never had a dog. How many dogs will you bring?" Gerald asked, suddenly interested.

"I'll probably bring twenty or so," August replied. "And twenty dogs are going to be a lot of work. I'll need extra help from you boys."

"Will we play with the doggies?" Phillip asked.

"Of course," August answered. "We'll give them lots of love and care every day. And we'll play with them and work with them. You'll see. It's going to be a great deal of fun."

"What about Momma?" Gerald questioned.

"Your Momma is going to have fun with the dogs, too," August said with a wink at Beth.

"And it won't be long, boys," Beth added, "before

you'll be ready to start learning to read and write."

"That's true," August agreed. "This roadhouse is going to need a lot of care, too. Your mother has already made long, long lists, so every day will hold plenty of things to keep us busy. And," August paused, looking purposefully into Beth's eyes, "I promise I'll never be away from here for any longer than I have to be, because I love you all so very much."

"We love you too, Daddy," Gerald said, glancing at his mother. "Momma said we could call you that, if you didn't mind."

August choked up from the emotion surging through his heart. "I would love it if you would call me Daddy," he replied. "I want very much to be the best daddy in the world to both of you."

The boys hugged him tightly around the neck, while August and Beth exchanged a look of love that bound them forever to one another. *God is so good,* August thought. In His perfect way, God had saved the best in life for the last, and August could not imagine a sweeter future.

"Why don't you boys go play for a little while? I need to talk with August—your dad—for a moment."

"But he just got home," Gerald protested.

"Can't we stay?" Phillip moaned.

"Now, boys," August said, putting them from his knee. "You must always mind your mother and me. Sometimes your safety or lives might depend upon it. Right now, your mom simply wants to talk to me, but obeying her is always important. Do you understand?"

The boys sobered at August's serious tone. "Yes, Daddy."

With a smile, August broke the somber moment. "Good. Now, you run play, and when I'm done talking to your mother, I'll come help you build something with your blocks."

The boys scampered off to their room, discussing at great length their plans for the toy building project.

"You have such a loving way with them," Beth remarked. "I'm amazed that you've never spent much time with children."

"There were never any around to spend time with. There was Julie, of course," he said referring to his sister, "but I was a child as well. I've always known, though, that I wanted to be a father. I've always wanted a house full of children and a home full of love."

"I feel like I've got so much to learn about you," Beth said wistfully. "You've never told me much about Nome or your sister. It's another part of you that I know nothing about."

August nodded. "Just remember, there's a great deal I don't know about you, either. But we have all the time in the world."

Beth frowned for a moment, remembering the war that engulfed the world. "It's a rather frightening time. The world is in such conflict. So many young men are dying to give us freedom and a future. It cuts my heart to imagine waving my sons off to war. I pray I never have to know that feeling."

"Yes," August said, remembering that he once wanted to be one of those marching away to war. "I've never looked at it quite that way. I was angry at God because He wouldn't let me be one of those going off to serve. I never thought of how it affected anyone but me. Now that two little boys I love could well face that responsibility, I feel the same way you do. I want to protect them and keep them far from the reaches of such a monster as war."

"Do you suppose the world will change so very much in the years to come? I mean after the fighting is over and the men have come home," Beth questioned.

"War always changes things," August said thoughtfully. "I remember reading about World War I. It seemed so far away and unimportant. Somebody else's war, I thought. Somebody else's land and people. But it wasn't that way, and neither is this. We're every bit as much a part of those who are fighting as they are of us. We give them a reason to fight, a reason to win. They need us, just as we need them."

"Is it selfish to want a good life with you and the boys, in the face of the adversity our soldiers are living with?" Beth inquired.

"I don't think so. I believe it's just as they would expect. Life goes on, and just as one war is over, another begins. Whether it's on a battlefield or in a hospital bed, it's a never-ending cycle, and God's hand is upon all," August replied.

"Then our destiny is in His hands, and nothing the world does or doesn't do will change that," Beth said with new certainty.

"That it is," August agreed and added, "A future with God's loving protection doesn't seem at all frightening."

Beth nodded and reached across the table for August's hand. His warm fingers wrapped around her own, and Beth knew there truly was nothing to

fear. With God and a good man at her side, the chal-
lenges of the world seemed to shrink under a shroud
of faith.

Destiny's road would be God's road, and though
the way might hold pitfalls and obstacles, Beth and
August would travel it together, always guided by
the Creator of it all.

A Letter To Our Readers

Dear Reader:

In order that we might better contribute to your reading enjoyment, we would appreciate your taking a few minutes to respond to the following questions. When completed, please return to the following:

Rebecca Germany, Editor
Heartsong Presents
P.O. Box 719
Uhrichsville, Ohio 44683

1. Did you enjoy reading *Destiny's Road*?
   ☐ Very much. I would like to see more books
      by this author!
   ☐ Moderately
      I would have enjoyed it more if _____

   _____

2. Are you a member of *Heartsong Presents*? Yes   No
   If no, where did you purchase this book? _____

   _____

3. What influenced your decision to purchase
   this book? (Circle those that apply.)

Cover	Back cover copy
Title	Friends
Publicity	Other _____

4. On a scale from 1 (poor) to 10 (superior), please rate the following elements.

___Heroine   ___Plot

___Hero   ___Inspirational theme

___Setting   ___Secondary characters

5. What settings would you like to see covered in *Heartsong Presents* books?

_____

_____

6. What are some inspirational themes you would like to see treated in future books?_____

_____

_____

7. Would you be interested in reading other *Heartsong Presents* titles?   Yes   No

8. Please circle your age range:

| Under 18 | 18-24 | 25-34 |
| 35-45 | 46-55 | Over 55 |

9. How many hours per week do you read? _____

Name _____

Occupation _____

Address _____

City _____ State _____ Zip _____

······ Hearts♥ng ······

HEARTSONG PRESENTS TITLES AVAILABLE NOW:

(If ordering from this page, please remember to include it with the order form.)

·········· Presents ··········

_HP43 VEILED JOY, *Colleen L. Reece*
_HP44 DAKOTA DREAM, *Lauraine Snelling*
_HP45 DESIGN FOR LOVE, *Janet Gortsema*
_HP46 THE GOVERNOR'S DAUGHTER, *Veda Boyd Jones*
_HP47 TENDER JOURNEYS, *Janelle Jamison*
_HP48 SHORES OF DELIVERANCE, *Kate Blackwell*
_HP49 YESTERDAY'S TOMORROWS, *Linda Herring*
_HP50 DANCE IN THE DISTANCE, *Kjersti Hoff Baez*
_HP51 THE UNFOLDING HEART, *JoAnn A. Grote*
_HP52 TAPESTRY OF TAMAR, *Colleen L. Reece*
_HP53 MIDNIGHT MUSIC, *Janelle Burnham*
_HP54 HOME TO HER HEART, *Lena Nelson Dooley*
_HP55 TREASURE OF THE HEART, *JoAnn A. Grote*
_HP56 A LIGHT IN THE WINDOW, *Janelle Jamison*
_HP57 LOVE'S SILKEN MELODY, *Norma Jean Lutz*
_HP58 FREE TO LOVE, *Doris English*
_HP59 EYES OF THE HEART, *Maryn Langer*
_HP60 MORE THAN CONQUERORS, *Kay Cornelius*
_HP61 PICTURE PERFECT, *Susan Kirby*
_HP62 A REAL AND PRECIOUS THING, *Brenda Bancroft*
_HP63 THE WILLING HEART, *Janelle Jamison*
_HP65 CROWS'-NESTS AND MIRRORS, *Colleen L. Reece*
_HP66 ANGEL FACE, *Frances Carfi Matranga*
_HP67 AUTUMN LOVE, *Ann Bell*
_HP68 DAKOTA DUSK, *Lauraine Snelling*
_HP69 RIVERS RUSHING TO THE SEA, *Jacquelyn Cook*
_HP70 BETWEEN LOVE AND LOYALTY, *Susannah Hayden*
_HP71 A NEW SONG, *Kathleen Yapp*
_HP72 DESTINEY'S ROAD, *Janelle Jamison*
_HP73 SONG OF CAPTIVITY, *Linda Herring*

Great Inspirational Romance at a Great Price!

Heartsong Presents books are inspirational romances in contemporary and historical settings, designed to give you an enjoyable, spirit-lifting reading experience. You can choose from 73 wonderfully written titles from some of today's best authors like Colleen L. Reece, Brenda Bancroft, Janelle Jamison, and many others.

When ordering quantities less than twelve, above titles are $2.95 each.